MW00423322

Last Call

Stranded in the Stars, Volume 1

Naomi Lucas

Published by Naomi Lucas, 2017.

LAST CALL

First edition. September 20, 2017.

Written by Naomi Lucas.

Last Call
Stranded in the Stars:
Book One

. . . .

By Naomi Lucas

. . . .

Chapter One:

. . . .

Allie was *cursed*.

Chilly, dark whispers urged her to succumb to her nightmares. She hugged her pathetic form and shivered, as the dark quiet of the cave seeped deep into her mind.

The sand storm had raged for days planetside and it had been one of the longest maelstroms she had seen. Allie knew what was going to happen next. If she could just dig the sand away from the small hole that dropped down into her cave...

Every time a sandstorm hit, a beautiful meteor shower followed soon after. Those showers were one of the only pleasures she had left in her lonely existence, and it felt like a reward for surviving the storm, for not being buried alive and crushed to death by sand, or for not starving during the duration.

Or being trapped in the dark.

The meteor showers on "*Hell-in-Space*," which is what she liked to call the planet, were different from any other she had witnessed in her short life. The meteors were a cacophony of colors that dashed, collided, and expanded in the sky. The rocks reacted when entering the atmosphere and lit up the world with a rippling cascade of colors, like fireworks during an Aurora Borealis.

The showers would last for hours, and their beauty was always equal to the strength of the storm that had caused them. She was desperate to dig out of her cave and see it.

Allie sighed as she ducked back into her space and grabbed an elongated piece of metal that she had salvaged long ago, then went back to work breaking through the entrance.

I'm buried in deep this time. If she had any hope left of rescue, she would have been terrified of being buried alive, but such primitive fears barely concerned her anymore. She had been in this exact situation numerous times before and had always come out alive in the end.

Any day could be her last on *'HIS,'* pronouncing it like a curse word, hissing like a feral cat. The only things that scared her these days were the giant snake-like monsters that lurked deep beneath the ground, and the thick, oppressive darkness.

In a rush, she attacked the dirt-packed barrier in her way. Stabbing at it, she put all of her strength into destroying the wall in front of her. She pretended it was that nasty bitch, Fate, as a deluge of golden sand poured past her feet.

Feeling angry, violent, and above all frustrated gave her the willpower to break through. Allie breathed in the small amount of satisfaction she got from exorcising her pain.

She knew that if she was left alone with her thoughts for too long, she would see every lifeless face from that day, when the transporter ship she had been on crash-landed on this rock many years ago.

Those faces haunted her thoughts and consumed her nightmares with waves of guilt and terror. She pictured the other desperate women in her bunker, the ones searching the stars for a better future where they weren't controlled by the Warlord's men, or any men for that matter.

She had been part of a group of women who were smuggled out of the radical Trentian-controlled territories. Territories that were on the fringes of every galaxy, so far away from any governing council that most weren't aware of their existence.

Allie was a coveted outcast where she grew up; the aliens both needed her and hated her as she had been the only unmated Earthian female of breeding age at the colony. It made her precious to the men but equally hated by the Trentian women.

When she turned fourteen cycles, she was required to go through elaborate, probing tests to determine whether she could be bred.

She wrapped her arms around her stomach as she remembered the hands and cold medical equipment exploring her genitalia. Groping her, making her feel like a piece of meat. Luckily for her she was deemed fruitful, and was sent away to the female-only community to be protected until it was her time to be paired with a warrior of the colony.

The impotent women had it the worst. They held no status in these fringe cultures and held even fewer rights. If they couldn't secure employment in service to breeders, they often ended up in pleasure domes. It was in this society that she had come of age. So technologically advanced and yet so primitive at the same time.

It was her species, the Earthians, who had made countless Trentian women barren.

When she had just turned seventeen cycles, after spending three years at the commune, a Trentian Warlord visited her and chose her for his wife. She remembered him clearly, a large male with black emotionless eyes and a shaved, glistening head.

The females of age were all made to stand in a line with nothing on but simple, sheer white gowns. As the perverted male went to each woman, he lifted her gown and checked her vaginal channel with his finger for her innocence. Allie recalled his finger pressing against hers painfully while tears slid down her face.

No male before had the right to touch them, but in such a primitive place the man with the black eyes had warred with the previous clan leader and won. He was accountable to no one on their small planet and was thought to be possessed with madness.

It was rumored that fertile women were in even shorter supply at their colony than was let on, and Allie could only imagine the stressful burden the Warlord bore, knowing that his warriors would someday not be replenished.

Shaking herself out of her thoughts, Allie set forth out of the cave and into the barren desert that was her home. As she sat down to catch her breath, she opened the food pouch attached to her ragged rope belt and picked a critter out to eat, directing her thoughts to a lighter subject. The meteor shower was in full effect above her.

Always in awe of its beauty, her mouth fell open as she watched the atmospheric gases in the sky move like an ocean amidst a gale. Blues and greens mixed with purples splashed with reds; the colors danced before her eyes. She had been the only survivor of the crash lucky enough to see this magical display.

To the right, over the sandy hills, far in the distance, the remnants of the transporter ship remained. She couldn't see it– being several days journey away– but she knew it could see her. It was a constant reminder of all the horrors she had escaped.

Only in very dire circumstances did she ever go back to the mausoleum. The wreckage was haunted by ghosts.

Something sparkled out of the corner of her eye in the opposite direction of the ruins—it was a meteor unlike any she had ever seen before. It glinted a silvery grey with red strips of light coming off the side; it wasn't moving like any other meteor, either.

Allie stood up and squinted at the foreign object as it became easier to discern. The silver arrow was coming closer to the planet surface and it hadn't dissipated into dust.

"It's a ship!" She gasped in awe. *Another ship is about to crash land onto 'HIS.'* Allie leapt up, forgetting about the meteor storm raging above her head and started moving in the direction of the descending spaceship.

Chapter Two:

. . . .

T*wo weeks.*

Jack had been pursuing this damned pirate captain for two fucking weeks, and he was almost impressed with the man for evading him for so long. But being dragged out to deep space irked him. Larik should fight him like a man instead of running like a coward.

He hadn't had a challenging fight in what seemed like decades. Not since the war.

He was a Cyborg, created for war, and when there was no war, what the hell did a Cyborg like Jack do? Hunt. But hunting wasn't the same as brutally ending a life, sinking your dagger into the enemy's neck, or shooting off his leg and leaving him to bleed to death. War was as bloody as it was sublime.

It had been decades since the galactic war over the homeland sector; the Earthian people and the Trentian aliens had fought ruthlessly for it. They originated from the same galaxy and evolved at a similar rate. Jack would have likened it to home turf and all but he hadn't been around for the beginning. Humanoids were irrational and fear could have played a big part.

The war had been long and brutal and had spanned nearly a century. At the beginning, Earthians had just discovered a method for galactic space travel, and it was at this crucial time of exploring, learning, and expanding that they encountered the Trentians. Both species possessed alpha tendencies, and those tendencies prevented either side from coming to an agreement.

The problem with two intelligent species interacting was that one had to dominate the other, and the best way to show dominance was through battle and bloodshed.

The war only ended once the Earthians and Trentians began to run out of resources. They'd invested too much in controlling a single sector of the universe that when galactic space travel became *inter*galactic, the borders had blurred. The losses incurred were monumental, and at a pivotal point before their mutual destruction, they realized that they could interbreed. It was from those unions and the many generations after that a peace agreement was made.

There wasn't much of a difference between the species. The Earthians were frailer but more level-headed, tactical, and calculating, while the Trentians were quick to action and overwhelming in their speed, wiry strength, and endurance.

The Trentians were often taller but were mainly distinguished by their hair and skin tones. They often had pale-white skin with equally light hair. It was their eyes that often gave them away, with colors that ranged from violet to turquoise; one could not reproduce them artificially.

Their home world, Xantaeus Trent, was farther from their sun and because of that they could survive in extremely cold conditions. They could tolerate a warm climate but not a hot one. In spite of that, they were far more resilient to environmental variations than Earthians. They could also see better in the dark.

Jack knew that Cyborgs like himself were walking, talking Earthian-made abominations. Perfectly designed to resemble intimidating human males and females– closely enough for subterfuge but distinct in their domineering aura and mannerisms. They represented a harmonious union between bio-organics and advanced cybernetic technology. They were new-age Frankenstein monsters.

The Earthians would have been obliterated if they hadn't created my brethren and me to level the playing field.

One part human, one part machine, grown in a vat that simulated a human female's womb. The Cyborgs had no parents, as they were a mixture of the very best Earthian genes, and were programmed for war.

Each Cyborg was unique with differing biomaterial makeups and mechanics. Some of them could move at light speed, some were given the mechanics to lift freight-trains, while others had such advanced processors that they could tactically predict the immediate future based on current events.

There was even rumor of a Cyborg that could access different dimensions and manipulate time, if those abilities were even possible. Jack didn't know. Theoretical studies remained theoretical and when it came to space, aliens, and time, those theories were often met with disbelief and skepticism until proven otherwise.

Jack, meanwhile, was designed to be a living computer virus, ever changing, ever evolving, and always one step ahead. He could connect to all manner of machines and take control. He could infect them with his nanobots and then track those bots all over the cosmos. Earthians and Trentians alike had tried to off him on numerous occasions, and even his own brethren were wary of him because he could corrupt their systems.

He had an ability that couldn't be limited, and so he couldn't be controlled. It was deemed an act of treason if he tracked, spied, or even so much as transmitted a single one of his bots into the government's network, be it on a single battleship or an encrypted computer. Because of this, he held no allegiance to anyone but himself.

And he had no problem being neutral. Jack didn't work with either side now that the war was over, and it never really mattered anyway; the species could breed together, muddying up any established species.

His machine side was reasonable and understood the fear, but his human side often wanted violence. Violence like wrapping his hands around Pirate Captain Larik's neck, breaking a few bones, then turning him in and collect his reward. He had never been one for patience.

Jack could just see his target's small flyer far in the distance, and what he couldn't see he could sense with his systems. The target's ship was flying close to Argo, a barren rock of a planet that had no resources. No resources meant no profit and no profit meant no colonization. It was an uncared for, forgotten frontier planet.

He connected back with his ship and pushed his impulse drives at the optimum speed to close the distance to Larik's ship. Once he got close enough, he could stunlock Larik's navigational system, infect it, take the ship over, and bring Larik in.

Jack was the best bounty hunter for a reason: he didn't have to move a single muscle to accomplish any of this.

If someone I was hunting would have run into the middle of a forest, I may have had difficulty locating them, but one would have to find a forest to run into first.

He was aware of his shortcomings. Luckily, few others were.

His reputation was renowned over several Earthian-controlled galaxies and even more Trentian controlled ones. He was a lone-wolf hunter for hire by anyone who had the money and the guts to contact him.

Humans were afraid of him and his fellow Cyborgs. At one point, the council tried to wipe out all of the war-created Cyborgs due to their violent tendencies and uncontrollable natures. They changed their minds quickly after he personally hacked their technology and turned it against them, and a fellow Cyborg, Breco, blew up a planet destroyer. Now there was a stiff yet reasonable working relationship with each side that only *occasionally* resulted in death.

Pirate Captain Larik, on the other hand, was not a Cyborg but a half-breed who happened to align with the Trentians.

He was wanted by the Earthian council to answer for crimes that included, but were not limited to, abducting Earthian females and trafficking them to Trent colonies for breeding, smuggling blacklisted items, for being an active member of the *Impure Gang*, for excessive use of hostile weaponry against the council, and leading an intergalactic syndicate. Larik had been a busy man.

When he smuggled the daughter of a high chancellor along with a handful of other high-ranking women to Xanteaus Trent, a crime considered so monstrous by Earthian purists, the council sought Jack specifically to apprehend Larik. They preferred him captured alive but would accept his corpse if it came to that.

He was gaining on the pirate and in just a few more clicks he'd have Larik's system under his control. The pirate was uncannily intelligent, though, and Jack knew he had a trick up his sleeve. His prediction came to fruition when he dipped closer toward Argo's innermost atmosphere.

Larik was leading him straight into a meteor storm.

The half-breed would rather face death than be captured by me. Going into the meteor storm would damage both ships, and Larik was either going to get very lucky or very dead.

Jack hailed Larik's ship, and after a moment a connection was made. He wondered if Larik knew that receiving his request through the network intercommunication channels would make it easier for him to overpower his ship's system.

I wonder if he even cares.

"You're going to get us killed," Jack hailed through as a faint static noise filled his usually quiet cockpit.

"It took you long enough to catch up to me, Cyborg. I expected more from the council's... *best*," a bored voice eventually answered. "Turn back if you're afraid of the falling rocks. No one's stopping you."

"Hmm, you'd like that, wouldn't you? To extend this damned cat and mouse chase a little longer?"

They weaved in synchronicity through the meteors that began to resemble raining gunfire. Jack was impressed with how the pirate evaded collisions as if the man had a sixth sense.

"How much are the bureaucrats paying you for my capture?"

"Enough."

Fearlessly, Jack flew right into the storm, wanting this shit show to end. He personally didn't give a damn about the pirate nor that he delivered breeders to the Trentians– the Trentian men wanted to procreate and they needed viable Earthian females to do that.

During a gruesome period of the war, biochemical weapons were released that made many members of the future generations of Trentian females impotent. It had been a sick thing for the Earthians to do, but he understood the tactical logistics and advantages of the move.

Besides, most Earthian females couldn't get to Trentian colonies fast enough; if they were virile, they were treated like queens. The half-breed children were beautiful.

"Oh come on, tell me. It's a matter of pride," Larik quipped through the intercom.

"A single ton of pyrizian ore."

The pirate didn't immediately respond and Jack thought it may be because of what the price of his head was worth.

"Damn."

Jack laughed at the expected response. Pyrizian ore was a very rare, very strong star ore that was often used to create powerful and advanced weaponry. It could only be found in fading white dwarfs, dead stars on their last stretch of life.

The meteor shower increased in intensity as they came closer to the planet's surface.

The effort Jack took to dodge the meteors caused him to lose any gain he had made on the pirate and Larik, the lucky bastard, was getting away. Right when he was about to make a final push to capture the flyer, a loud noise permeated the air and in that moment all his systems went red.

Cursing, he diagnosed that a football-sized meteor had crashed into his right drive. The colloid silver nanoparticles that his ship was using to manage variations in temperature couldn't keep up with the shifts.

He wasn't going to lose his ship, and a repair could easily be made, but he was going to drastically lose speed.

Jack repositioned himself to use his body as an energy source and forced his ship into overdrive, making one last push to get close enough to Larik. He wouldn't last long as a battery but he may still get the job done today.

It was then, during several critical seconds and closing in on success, that his ship was struck again. *What the hell was that?* He found no readings on the second impact and had no choice but to give up the chase, to land, and repair his ship.

He watched as the pirate ascended into the sky and flew away, the communication link disconnecting after a faint taunting laughter snaked through the intercom.

Grudgingly, he changed course to land on the rock called Argo.

• • • •

JACK MANEUVERED HIS vessel as carefully as possible, reflexively scanning all meteor activity happening around him. Slowing down and then abruptly picking up speed while zigzagging left and right, he felt like he was still dancing through a rain of bullets like he had done often during his war days.

He was almost in the clear, dipping into Argo's atmosphere where the meteors reacted and turned back into meaningless specks of dirt. The chemical reactions that were happening outside his ship were briefly intriguing but he soon lost interest as he descended to the ground.

This planet will do just fine.

He scanned everything for miles in every direction from his location. There was less life here blipping on his radar than a graveyard on Earth. He could immediately sense the giant behemoth wurms deep under the outer crust of the planet.

Those fuckers are big. His scans indicated that the monsters were sensitive to light and that he would have to remember to take extra precautions at night. Strangely enough, he could sense one moving life form, an anomaly, that was traveling toward his ship on the surface. It didn't appear to be a threat, but he decided to examine the life form further.

... A lone female. He took his attention away from the giant bugs under the planet's surface and solely focused on the girl moving his way. *This is an interesting development... how does a female end up on a rock like this?*

He could tell from analyzing her movements, heat signature, and heart rate that she was young and had to be Earthian. Unlike any other female he had encountered in the past, this one was alone and unprotected.

The closer she came to his ship, the more he could sense her presence, her erratic heartbeat, and her uniquely scented pheromones.

It must be something on this planet.

The surface climate was hot and dry, a blistering, undisturbed heat that sat stagnant over the landscape. *The female would have to be Earthian to withstand this amount of heat and lack of water.* Jack could sense an underground network of springs below the planet surface but no bodies of water above ground or clouds in the sky to indicate a change in weather.

He decided to dedicate half of his processors, which he knew was overkill, to track her movement while he went about preparing his ship for maintenance. He reconnected himself to his flyer and ran several diagnostic reports on all his ship's vital parts.

Filing away the pieces that needed to be repaired, he realized that he would have to salvage metal from other parts of his flyer to properly repair the damage to his impulse drives. It frustrated him to think that he would have to harvest from his own ship.

The girl must have come from somewhere. Maybe he could take what he needed from her vessel so he wouldn't have to take apart his. His ship was his home, an extension of himself, and taking apart hers would teach her the age old lesson about *survival of the fittest.*

Scanning the rest of the planet's surface nearby, he found no other heat sources, or other recently active ships.

The female may be just as stranded as I am right now, or maybe her ship has heat signature cloaking. Shit, for all he knew there could be a hidden colony of humans thriving here and she was sent forth as a trap.

The girl was close enough now to his location that she would be able to see his ship and its minor details. Her heat signature had stopped moving and he could tell she was now crouched down between the rocks and dunes outside.

Jack decided it was a great time to leave his ship and get a visual on his drives. He headed to the hatch and opened the capsule door to step out.

A blast of dry heat assailed him. *It's a fucking wasteland.*

Straight ahead of him was a desert that gradually turned into a forest of rocks that morphed into giant dull brown mountains in the distance. There was no color on this planet other than every shade and hue of brown. The only thing that could make this rock a paradise for him was a splattering of blood red and an active battlefield. His favorite color and pastime.

Above him, the meteor shower was ending and the vibrant colors were fading away. Jack pretended he didn't know she was there as he casually looked around at the terrain, covertly keeping an eye in the direction of the female and wondering what move she would make.

After several minutes of waiting for her reaction, he gave up and half turned toward his ship to assess the damage.

Chapter Three:

. . . .

It had taken her hours but she had finally managed to get within viewing distance of the ship. Excitedly, Allie realized that this had been her most interesting day since leaving the crash site to venture out into the planet; each day that preceded that terrifying one had been a stale existence, a blur of days, weeks, months, years of just surviving, of having no hope of rescue.

The day hadn't been a complete loss, though.

She had been fortunate to find sustenance several times over the course of the afternoon, and today she had located over half a dozen dead baby wurms along the ground. The wurms were a source of food on this planet, even though the thought of eating them still disgusted her.

They resembled grubs but had a milky white sheen to them, and in the sunlight they had a purple glisten. It was that sparkle that made it them easy to spot, and after a sandstorm the little dead bugs were everywhere, having been picked up by the wind and dying during the turbulence of the storm.

They were the spawn of the giant monsters just below the surface. There was some macabre satisfaction that the giant beasts below her were also her main source of food.

She shivered to herself.

She didn't eat the worms often: she couldn't, she never found enough to fully sustain her. But she found herself actively looking for the carcasses every time she went out to forage, and luckily her main source of food came from other tiny critters and dried out, chunky roots she found under rocks near the mountain range.

It was a day trip to get to the mountain range and back, so she only went as often as she needed to as the trek led her closer to the ghostly tomb.

Satisfied with her find today, she settled in to survey the ship in the distance.

The ship hadn't crashed like her transporter vessel but haltingly landed instead, disturbing nothing but the sand it packed into the ground. She had expected it to resemble the crumpled metal of the crash site of her flyer but it was unlike it in every way. She concluded that any supposed victims were most likely alive and well.

I haven't encountered another human in so long.

Allie now felt deeply insecure in her decision to investigate the ship. *What if the beings on board were loyal to the Warlord?* Or what if they were men just like him and his generals? The Warlord had never pursued the vessel she had been on, nor did he come after the maidens while they were still planetside. Why would he be here now?

Feeling her stomach sink, she quietly reached in her pouch and pulled out another root to munch on. The ship was unlike any she had seen before and she eyed it appreciatively; she could salvage a lot from its hull. If the beings on board didn't kill her first.

It was sleek, beautiful, and had a chrome gleam to it with streaks of red lights along the sides and above the lights large, tinted viewing glass ran along its entire frame. There was a dome at the top that was all glass, or some other substance that could withstand space travel.

She could just imagine the supplies such an expensive ship would have inside: cloth, tools, food, soap... She groaned to herself. *What I would do for a bar of soap.*

Her thoughts were abruptly cut off when the back capsule of the ship smoothly opened up.

She held her breath, waiting for something to happen, nervously running her fingertips through her mess of windblown hair. It was a couple of heart-pounding seconds before a figure slowly emerged. A man, a very large, lethal looking man. Allie felt her stomach dip further.

She zeroed in on his movements as he surveyed the terrain, his head cocked up, legs slightly apart, exuding an aura that screamed he owned everything he saw before him.

Good thing he can't see me.

When he turned in her direction, she slowly pushed herself closer to the ground in case she hadn't been entirely hidden. Her heart pounded as she tried to relax. Her long brown hair, the thinning leather rags she called clothing, and tanned skin camouflaged her perfectly on *Hell-in-Space*.

The strange male turned back toward his ship and she let out the long tense breath that she had kept in.

He must be looking at the damage. Maybe his ship was also caught in the meteor storm, like mine. She couldn't really tell from this distance.

Feeling equal parts curious and courageous, she moved forward, desperate to see the male up close.

She crouched behind a small rock outcropping that was several dozen yards closer to the male. He didn't look like a

Trentian. He resembled more of an Earthian but much larger. Berating herself, she knew she was putting herself in serious danger being this close but at the same time she knew she had little left to live for and that truth stopped her from retreating.

She assessed the risks: he could hurt her, kill her, or even steal her away and return her to the Warlord. He could also do much worse. But refusing to stay on that train of thought, she was satisfied that she was close enough to make out the details of his character.

He was the most frightening male she had ever laid eyes upon in her life. The male was tall enough to climb and every inch of his length was protected by hard black body armor with accentuations of dark grey mesh that sculpted around his muscles. He wore heavy boots that were rimmed with metal.

But what was most unnerving was the giant gun strapped across his back, the dual laser pistols on his tool belt, and the daggers strapped to his legs. He was not a simple man but a weapon-heavy warrior.

The man had strong features, a strong chin, high sculpted cheekbones, and all of it was oddly, perfectly symmetrical. The only imperfections he had were two scars: one that had split his bottom lip on his left side that descended towards his neck, and the other was just over his left eyebrow.

And his eyes... his eyes were silver and violent. Even from a distance, his eyes held a storm of dark emotions raging through them. She could only imagine how many beings died before them. If she could just get a closer look, she imagined she could see the gateway to hell and the souls of a thousand beings swimming behind them.

The male equally terrified and intrigued her.

She couldn't help the strange heat that pooled between her legs or the perspiration beading between her breasts. Her heart felt like thunder in her chest.

• • • •

JACK WENT ABOUT HIS ship, taking visuals of the damage and storing it in his database. A big damn meteor had struck his ship, not only fucking up the impulse drive but leaving jagged skid marks along the outer body.

Catching Larik wasn't just a job anymore. It was revenge. The bounty he would get for his capture would more than cover the cost of repairing the perforations, but that was just a bonus now.

The satisfaction of dumping his body on Taggert, a prisoner planet, with his blood still on his hands would be the real reward.

The pirate will pay for the crimes he committed against me.

Jack didn't give a damn about his other transgressions; it was personal now.

He breathed in deeply. Trying to calm himself down only ended up being a terrible mistake. The female had moved dangerously close to him. If he focused, he could hear her slight breaths. The wild girl either liked what she was seeing or was frightened because her heart rate had increased dangerously. A human male could have smelled the fear and pheromones wafting from her.

Groaning in frustration, Jack zeroed his attention in on the girl behind him, only putting up the pretense now about his ship.

Her breathing was elevated, her heat signature knocking up a degree. He could smell the sweat moistening her skin. It wasn't a bad smell. It was wild and erotic and drew him to the conclusion that this girl had been stranded on the planet for some time.

His mission was now buried deep in the recesses of his mind because his body was reacting to her smell, and even as a Cyborg his cybermechanics couldn't extract the pull she created. It would have been humbling, knowing the part of him that made him a man had more control over his technology, but he had a job to do and within the last hour he was beginning to change his priorities.

His bots were not doing a damn thing to cool his fascination. *How the hell was she exuding such powerful pheromones?* Nothing in his databases had an explanation.

He entertained the idea of walking over to her, lifting her in his arms and confronting her when the ground began to shake. A wurm passed dangerously close by beneath his feet. Taking his knife out for good measure, he stabbed the ground, knowing the vibrations would be felt by the monster. One of them had to act civilized.

Jack looked up. The meteor shower that caused this predicament was now over and Argo's sun was on its descent into darkness.

He made one last perusal of his ship, absently wiping some the dust that already started to collect on it and headed back to the hull. The monsters inhabiting this planet will be making their presence known and he didn't feel like tussling with one tonight.

He left the hatch open to his ship and waited in the shadows to see what the wild girl would do. If she were smart, she would take her leave while she still could.

Chapter Four:

. . . .

The male was naive.

He barely acknowledged the environment after his first survey of the terrain, and he could have been attacked and killed many times over if it had been night. Allie was always aware of her surroundings.

He even left his dagger in the sand.

She wanted to take it but knew he would miss it come morning.

She wanted to warn him, wanted to tell him of the monsters that came out after dark, especially since he blatantly left the hatch to his ship open. His actions were dangerous to his being. Allie mulled it over and decided she would wait awhile longer to see if he would come back out. It didn't hurt to play sentinel for a short time.

When it began to appear that he had retired for the day, Allie determined it was for the best that she retired too. The temperature was beginning to drop and it was always cold at dusk and even colder at night.

She judged the sun's location and, if she ran, she would make it back to her *hole-in-the-ground* before everything was consumed by the chilly darkness. She really shouldn't have stayed so long to watch him. Giving the open hatch one last look, Allie headed home.

At full sprint, an hour and a half later, she saw her sanctuary come into view. The exertion it took her to get back before dark caused her to nearly pass out, and it didn't help that she hadn't eaten more than one critter all day and was now faced with the repercussions, the weakness. She set aside her pouch, disrobed her rags, and slowly descended into the small warm spring at the back of her cave.

Years ago, when she found this place, she had cried for joy and stayed in the spring for a week, living here ever since and finally cutting off all ties with the tomb in which she had arrived.

The only light she had was from the tiny little organisms that lived at the bottom of the spring.

Once she had tried to capture them and bring them above water, only to fail when they all died soon after. Now she left them alone. They gave off just enough blue luminescence to discern the shapes of the rocks and her personal items around her.

She didn't have much, not after being stranded on this planet for a countless amount of time. Her makeshift home had an array of frayed cloth that she had brought with her, small metal brackets and pieces that had broken off of the ship when it first crashed here, and small bone tools that she had fashioned from the exoskeletons of long dead wurms.

Allie had several other worthless belongings, things that reminded her of civilization that she couldn't bring herself to get rid of. Her favorite of those pieces was an old, worn lighter that she had used up many moons ago. Now, when she felt wistful and bored, she would roll the spring with her thumb and listen to the soft zing.

Resting her head on the ledge, she wiggled her feet amongst the organisms beneath her and whispered to herself, "No shame..." then slid her hand between her legs.

Passion had been strictly forbidden at the commune as the crones drilled into her that it should be reserved only for breeding. The elder women of the group had ingrained the idea that there was perfection in innocence, sublimation in mating, and an extreme importance in sustaining the race.

The stress and the pressure that she had been under, mixed with the hatred from many of the other women she had lived with, had worn her down as she struggled to assimilate. No matter how often she reassured herself that the elderly women's mantra no longer applied, she always woke up the next morning feeling guilty.

A man had never excited her like the one who had stepped out of the ship today, and she wasn't entirely sure why. She didn't think it could be that he was the first man she had seen since her time traveling space, but something about the mere presence of him had caused her stomach to clench and her mouth to water.

Even now with her core tensing and burning up, she felt wanton shame.

Her entire body felt like a furnace as the pebbles beneath her butt dug in, her bare heels grinding into the slick ground.

Allie was attuned to everything around her– wanting to rub her body against the hard rocks of the spring and to imagine those rocks were the large male she had spied on all day. He had looked fierce and strong, and not just physically. His smoky eyes had been intense and discerning as he had scouted the area around his ship, and that natural strength drew her like a moon moth to a flame.

Maybe he intrigues me so much because it is strength that I am lacking.

She spread her legs open under the water as she thought about him and tickled her fingers between her legs. She continued her fantasy that it was his body that she pressed against– that he was impossibly large and anchoring her body like he owned it– like he owned everything he had lay his eyes on.

I want him to own me. I want something more than my imagination. This is my curse for running away, from not fulfilling my duties, for being the only one to survive.

She moaned as she brought herself to the first climax of the night– then she mewed again and again until she passed out to the thought of violent eyes penetrating her soul while he mated her into unconsciousness.

• • • •

JACK COULDN'T FOCUS. He repeatedly attempted to get his processors online to hunt for leads on Larik, but his attention kept going back to the female that had watched him all day.

She hadn't taken the bait and entered his ship. He was unsurprised. Only an idiot would. Oddly, though, he was disappointed that she hadn't.

He could tell that the female's movement had stopped because her heat signature had remained in the same place for the last hour. He was glad to know where she resided during the night, storing the information for later. Unfortunately, he could also tell that the signature was erratic, surmising that she may have been ill.

Jack would have liked the opportunity to get a visual of her, but the phantom version of her that he created in his mind would just have to be faceless tonight. That phantom smelled like sweat and sex and he pictured his fantasy kneeling between his legs with her mouth on his cock– sucking him off as if she were starving. Grunting with the lurid thought, he gripped his cock and started to work it with speed.

He increased his pumping, inhaling the lingering scent of her smell in the air. *Fuck.* He stood up, opened the hull and walked outside wearing nothing but a dagger strapped to his bicep. He continued walking until he stood over the area where she had crouched all afternoon.

Picturing her still there, looking down on her, he fucked his hand vigorously. He imagined that she was unaware of him while he jerked off above her. Her ass was in the air and it was a perfect apple shape, and she was touching herself. Spilling his seed all over the ground, he envisioned it spraying over her skin, surprising her, while it dripped between her legs and down her thighs, laying his claim on her.

What is wrong with me? I want to see my cum drip over her skin and I don't even know what she looks like. I'm acting like a savage.

He enjoyed the smell of his seed mixed with her fading scent, breathing in deeply several times and when he began to feel calm, he walked back to his ship and entered the lavatory to sanitize himself.

He had been taking job after job for so many years that he had never stopped to take a lover. He would have to remedy that, although finding a willing woman who was also sincere in her desire would be difficult. Jack couldn't stand the actresses that he had often encountered.

Thankfully, he did enjoy his fantasies knowing that he was as hard in bed as he was brutal in the battlefield, and most of the women he had met throughout the years during the fallout were often terrified of him, knowing what he was.

It was then that the ground began to shake again as a behemoth emerged nearby and let out a roar that would frighten grown, battle-hardened men. His thoughts drifted away from his disappointing sexual conquests and instead towards the creature staking its territory, waiting for it to move on.

After he dressed and strapped his weapons back on, he exited his ship and headed in the direction of the girl. If she was ill, he wanted to know. His human side was still susceptible to disease and he didn't want whatever she had. His body was not at optimum function after the landing.

Jack kept his pace fast. The stars were bright enough that he didn't need to switch to his night vision and it wasn't long before he was standing several yards from the girl's signature; he could hear her heart beating now if he focused on it. She was below him and he easily found the small hole that led to her rocky, underground hideout.

Her breathing was soft and even, so he jumped down silently, pulling out a syringe-like device strapped to his hip. The space was small and it glowed with a dim indigo blue throughout. He heard the small water source tucked into a corner and walked over to it to lean over the still pool.

The light originated from deep beneath the glassy water; he knelt down and reached out. The water was lukewarm to the touch and relatively clean. It came from a spring deep underground.

Jack turned toward the girl sleeping on the ground, monitoring her physiological patterns to ensure he wasn't going to wake her up. She was facing away from him.

Quietly, he brushed her hair to the side and pricked the skin behind her ear; her body flinched slightly from the sting before it settled back into sleep. The syringe administered a weak sedative in case things went sour.

He stabbed his finger with the same syringe and ran a diagnosis, finding nothing life-threatening. Afterwards, he had his nanocells clear her out of his system. She was malnourished and was on a terrible diet but nothing indicated illness or disease. Jack couldn't see what she looked like accurately in the dark even though he had night vision and his need to see her increased with his disappointment.

He turned to leave for his ship but stopped short, looking around her home again, noticing she had very little. He could give her so much with so few of his supplies. He reached down and grabbed a threadbare cloth and draped it over her form before turning back to climb out of her space.

Without giving it another thought, he successfully reconnected to the underground telecom channels as he jogged back to his ship and processed all the new information he could find on Larik; he worked on his mission for the remainder of the night.

• • • •

JACK WAS GETTING ANNOYED. After spending the remainder of the rest cycle monitoring channels, which ended up being a waste of time, he had no new leads.

It was light out now. The sun had risen several hours prior and was going to reach its zenith soon and since he rose that morning, he had been repairing his ship, willing his body to replenish so the repairs would go faster.

There hadn't been any sign of the female since yesterday evening. His sensors told him she had yet to leave her cave and that her breathing was even. He figured she was a late sleeper or that the sedative he gave her had been too strong.

Frustrated in more ways than one, he focused on the job before him, scorching off a damaged part of his impulse drive. The outside only had cosmetic damage; it was the interior that was knocked up. *My poor baby*. He patted the smooth metal. Soon he would have the palladium circuitry exposed to work on. The process would take some time but he would get it done. It wasn't like it was his first time performing surgery on the flyer.

Putting his laser gun aside, he removed another panel of the outer shell, placing it with the rest that came before and got his first view of what awaited him. The circuits didn't look damaged. They just appeared to be burned out. If he wasn't a Cyborg that could connect with machines, he may have never known there was a problem here.

Reaching in and pinching one of the square blue and red circuits between his finger and thumb, he began to directly transfer nanobionics into it. The bionics would heal the circuits as if it were a bio-organic organism.

He used those same nanobots to infect, take over, and destroy machines as well. The only drawback was how long the process would take. Jack only had so many bots that he could use at a given time before his body needed to create more.

A ship as advanced as his baby had a lot of variable chemical reactions his bots would have to morph and adapt to.

Glancing up, the sun was now directly above him, and pulling away from the impulse drive he scanned for the female's presence again– she was moving, and in his direction. Smirking, he shed his chest armor, unstrapping the weapon belts attached across his back and chest, only leaving his bicep straps in place. *I am a scarred motherfucker.* He had white streaks crisscrossing all over his body. Most women were disturbed by them while others, the wanton ones who had seen him naked, wanted to add more.

He wanted to know how the wild girl would react to them. Wiping the back of his hand across his mouth, he went back to work.

• • • •

ALLIE WOKE UP SORE and dirty and gingerly opened up her eyes while sitting up. She had passed out again on the floor– never making it to her bedding in the corner. Dust specks floated in the air around her, silhouetted against the ray of light beaming through the cave entrance. She could tell it was late morning.

Moving over to the spring, she quickly submerged her body in the water, scrubbing the dirt and sweat that caked her skin, dunking her head under several times to rinse her hair. Satisfied, she got out to pick up her leather rags and dress and wrapped the frayed cloth around her breasts, around her waist and between her legs, and several times around her feet.

She stuffed a handful of roots into her mouth and climbed out of her cave, eagerly jogging in the direction of the newcomer while absently scratching her neck. *Please let him still be here.*

The anxiety she felt didn't last long when she rounded a boulder and saw the glint of chrome in the distance. Moving closer, Allie noticed the hatch to the ship was open and unattended and that the dagger from last night was still hilt-deep in the ground.

There were guns, body armor, and straps piled up next to the dagger. She peered around warily before crouching low to the ground to look closer. The male's footprints were scattered all along the side of his ship, especially near an open metal plate.

He must have been at it all morning. Where is he now? There were fresh footprints leading away from the vessel but she couldn't be sure if he was actually gone.

Deciding to follow them for a short while, she soon realized that he really had left as they kept going out into the distance. She took the opportunity that this presented, turned back towards the ship, and ducked through the hatch.

If I'm quick enough, I can find supplies and be gone before he returns. She steeled her nerves and ventured forward.

Immediately upon entering the hull, the atmosphere changed. Inside the temperature was comfortable where just moments ago it had been a dry, heavy heat. The air, she sniffed, smelled clean and metallic.

She looked around curiously while proceeding, as everything was sleek, dark, and pristine. Unlike her cave dwelling in every way, there were no dust specks floating in the air. *I'm the dirtiest thing in this place. He's going to know someone has been here.*

Moving forward with apprehension, she entered a large round room.

I must be in the center.

There was a circular table directly in the middle and central to that was a floating planet. Awed, she moved closer to examine it. The planet was a beautiful holographic sphere with equal parts blue and green. Thinking to herself, *this must be a planet with oceans and vegetation*. Earth came to mind. Allie had learned of her ancestors' home world while part of the Trentian colony. One of the elder women, whose mate had long since passed, had known people from Earth.

Allie didn't know where her ancestors came from because she never knew her family. Her mother's mate had dropped her off at an orphanage before she could remember, as was prudent to do at the colony. Females were to be monitored and protected and one man wouldn't have been able to do it alone.

She looked straight ahead past the floating planet and found the cockpit; she could even see the outside, the hot barren landscape, through the viewing screens. Two symmetrical corridors were located on either side of her.

If this room was ever to be closed off and she spun in place for several seconds, there would have been no way to tell which door led to what area. She knew she had gotten distracted and quickly picked the path to her right, hoping to encounter the medical bay or lavatory.

Instead, she found herself in a small, enclosed space that housed soft white walls with pillow-like protrusions. She reached out to touch one, her finger softly indenting into the cushioned frame. She looked around at the padded room as even the ceiling resembled the walls and the only abnormality was the hardness of the floor.

There were no windows and the only light came from the small rim of a soft white circular orb above her head. Allie didn't like the strangeness of the room or the stark, austere nature of it. Space reminded her of nightmarish past events; she turned around to leave.

As she left the room she heard heavy footsteps, the noise shocking her system. In a frightened rush, she quickly went back into the padded room and hid next to the entrance, her body flush with the soft wall. She placed a hand over her mouth to keep herself from gasping out a sound as her other hand gripped her wrist to keep it in place.

The footsteps got louder as they entered the center of the ship. She heard shuffling and then a muffled clang as if something had been dropped. Her eyes closed as a chair from the middle table scraped across the floor. The next few sounds were indiscernible. The man was doing something at the table.

Allie felt as though she had been standing there, holding her breath, for what seemed like forever before she heard the man get up and move away, his footsteps receding further into the ship. She softly let go of her breath and peeked around the corner. The room before her was empty but the table was not.

It was covered with metal bits and tools, most likely pieces from the ship or items used to repair it. Shuffling silently into the room and placing her body close to the outer walls, she kept a watchful eye on where the footsteps had disappeared. She stood there for a minute, listening for any sign that he may come back. When it remained silent, she approached the table to examine the items he had dropped.

Everything before her looked foreign. She wasn't about to swipe something that may alert him of her presence and the items on the table looked important. There was even a small gun of some sort; she ran her fingers over the chilled, silvery metal. She could see the reflection of the holographic planet on it before dropping her hand away.

If I stay any longer, I will get caught. Taking her chances, she quietly walked back toward the hatch, holding her breath the entire time.

When she stepped back into the arid heat and the crunch of dirt sounded beneath her feet, she ran from the ship, back toward the safety of her cave.

The beautiful gun was now a deadly reminder imprinted into her mind.

• • • •

JACK LEARNED A LOT about the girl when she didn't snatch any of the precious things he had left on the table. Some of the machinery he had placed out was priceless. The gun, one of his most coveted and prized possessions, was made from pyrizian rock. He had also left out communication devices, schematics, tools, and medicinal products and the girl had snatched none of it.

Instead, as he followed her trail, she had gone into the brig. He could still see the small finger indent she had left in the wall. It looked queer amongst the bright austere walls.

So she wasn't here to pillage my valuables. But she was willing to invade his space and encroach on a battle flyer.

He now knew the girl had no idea that he was a Cybernetic organism.

The next day he purposely left the hatch open but instead of placing random valuables out, he created food from his replicator and opened his supply unit. He placed the breaded rations on a random panel in his cockpit and then left his ship, curious to see what the girl would do with the sustenance.

He approached the burned out circuitry that was now slowly repairing itself and transferred more of his nanobots into it. He did this every day to speed up the process, but his patience was running thin. Every hour he was stuck was another hour that Larik had to find a hole to hide in. He ground his teeth before forcing his body to shut down his frustration.

After he finished up, feeling slightly faint from losing so many nanobots in such a short amount of time, he walked away from his ship to monitor the girl at a distance.

It didn't take long for her to appear, her movements and body language bolder as she began to feel more comfortable with the daily routine. He watched, pleased, as she tracked his footsteps again.

He still couldn't make out definitive features about her but he did notice her long golden brown hair and her small frame. She had stopped to stare at his prints fading into the distance, to where he was located now but she didn't move. Instead, she stared in his direction as if she could tell he was there.

What the hell? Jack now felt he had to be the one to remain frozen and even out his breathing, trying not to alert her.

He watched in frustration as she turned around and fled.

Chapter Five:

• • • •

Allie had returned the next day, not to explore his ship but to confront the strange man. It had taken her hours to build up the courage but as she approached the ship, he wasn't there, his footprints leading out into the landscape again.

Why did he keep going out into a wasteland that had nothing? She had gotten an uneasy feeling, losing all of her courage in the process and quickly left. She hadn't seen him since that first day but desperately wanted to look at him again. The fact that the scenario happened twice now felt like a sign that she should be wary.

I haven't survived this long without listening to my sense.

Allie returned to watch him the following several days but hadn't found him at the ship again. She could tell progress was being made on the repairs; the plating around the damage had begun to change and some of the discarded slats on the ground had been removed and reused on the area where the long jagged laceration had been. The worst of it was covered up now.

The next day the routine continued. When the ship seemed abandoned again and the man was nowhere to be found, she felt her courage return to enter the vessel. The hatch was always open and the last few days she had watched for him for several hours but he had never appeared.

She would have time to look around and the thought of soap gave her enough courage and excitement to urge her on. He wouldn't miss soap.

Allie gingerly stepped out of her hidden spot within the rocks and dunes and advanced toward the sleek ship. A wave of adrenaline washed over her as a strange and terrible hold squeezed her heart. She placed her fisted hand where it hurt and willed it away, refusing to acknowledge it.

Today she would make her own choices.

She entered the hatch and cautiously walked down the long glistening corridor toward the spacious circular room with the floating planet. Heading in the opposite direction from the strange white space, she found an open panel that hadn't been there before. Listening intently, she couldn't hear any sound but her beating heart. When she felt it was safe enough to investigate, Allie entered the new room and found a supply closet.

The splash of colors, strange shapes, and exotic products overwhelmed her. On one shelf she saw tinted crystal tubes filled with colored liquids, large clear packages filled with brittle, grainy substances, and another shelf held disks, plates, and myriad strange devices.

One entire wall was a powerful door, outlined in glowing red and blue with an intricate lock system. She wondered what could be behind such a large barrier as nothing else she had seen on the ship looked as menacing or secure, not even the hatch. Allie reached out to touch one of the framed glowing colors when she heard footsteps.

"What do you think you're doing?" A deep voice sounded directly behind her, stopping her hand in midair. Terrified that she was trapped, Allie couldn't bring herself to look.

A loud bang went off as something was dropped nearby, and she jumped in surprise when a large hand encasing her forearm jerked her to face the man who held her.

Violent grey eyes filled her vision. The hand on her arm felt like heated steel.

"I asked you a question. Can you even speak?" He demanded, looking angrier by the second. He was gripping both of her arms now and lifting her up just enough that she had to point her toes down to keep her balance.

They stayed that way for what seemed like forever, staring at each other. Her heart had stopped. She was frightened by his eyes because it felt like he was stealing her soul. His face had darkened into a hard, determined expression as her gaze wavered to his mouth. Shivering, she wetted her lips. "Y-yes. I can speak," she whispered. He released her suddenly, and she nearly fell.

The male moved away from her to pull out a chair from the central table. Turning it to face her, he sat down, not once looking away. "You're either very brave or incredibly stupid. Trespassing on a highly weaponized battle flyer, completely alone and from what I can tell, unarmed," he perused her body, "and barely dressed."

"Are you going to hurt me?" She asked quietly. Had she made a mistake in coming here?

"Yes. Unless you give me a reason not to."

Shaking to herself, she did feel incredibly stupid. There was no way this man wasn't aware of everything that was happening at any given moment. *I bet he even saw me enter his ship.*

"Please..." she lied, "I was just trying to help. You had left your ship open and there– there are monsters here. I– I wanted to help," she broke eye contact with him, staring at the scar on his lip instead. "You never came back to your ship."

He laughed at her, "You were trying to help me?" The man retorted sarcastically. "Look at me, girl, I need no help, from anybody. Especially from someone like you– a defenseless waif with no weapon nor sense." He said as he unbuckled his gun belt, making a show of placing the gun on the table in front of her. Feeling intimidated, Allie couldn't help but notice his hands, remembering what she had thought of them several nights ago. "What's your name?"

Still watching his hand as he rested it under his chin, settling his elbow over his knee. She forgot the question. "What?" She asked.

"Your. Name?" he repeated slowly.

An embarrassing flush heated her cheeks, knowing that she looked like a simpleton but she couldn't help it. He was the first human she had come in contact with in many solar cycles.

"Allie," she whispered.

The man shifted forward on his chair at her answer. "Hmm, Allie. That sounds Earthian. Are you Earthian?"

"Yes," she said softly, looking up into his eyes again. He was still staring at her with fiery intensity, and his gaze was beginning to burn.

"That's very interesting, Allie. You see, this is a Trentian controlled space sector. Billions of miles off the grid and billions more from the nearest Earthian colony. How the hell does an Earthian female get all the way out to the fringes, alone, on Argo?" He continued, "Where's your space ship? My scanners don't detect one. Lie to me and I will hurt you," he growled.

"I don't have a ship. I was on a transporter ship. Long ago. We were headed to the metropolis, Espara..." She trailed off.

"And... that doesn't answer my question."

Allie shook herself internally. "Something happened, something bad. I don't know what exactly. It was all so fast but I believe the ship malfunctioned and it was horrible. We had the taste of freedom one moment and then the next, we were on a collision course towards the planet surface– I was the only one to survive." She felt her words stumble out.

* * * *

JACK DIDN'T KNOW WHY he cared but he could see the pain in her eyes, and he wanted to make that pain go away. *She needs a protector.* He stared at her, taking her in, committing her to memory.

He knew his silence was scaring her and he could tell by the pretty pink flush to her skin that his examination wasn't going unnoticed. He was frightening her on purpose and began to regret it. He had a feeling that it was the wrong approach in dealing with her. His logical side won out: he knew this girl was not here by design, she was not here in sedition.

What a wild looking girl he had in his midst. Her hair was long and tangled, the strands not able to decide whether to curl into ringlets, plaster against her skin, or fall loosely down her body.

It was a pretty shade of golden brown and he imagined grabbing it, forcing her to look at him, watching her large vulnerable eyes widen and her mouth making a pretty 'O.'

The ringlets that framed her face called to him. His fingers wanted to play with the fallen curls.

Her body was on display for him, her clothing nothing more than rags tied around her chest, waist, and feet. He knew he would have to give her something better to wear. Her waist was much too small but it did fan out nicely into curvy hips. If she would just turn around and take off her clothes, he bet that ass would have been a heart.

Jack couldn't help but appreciate her shape– toned, small, with long legs. He pictured her in a dozen different positions.

Lust speared through him: she was a dream, better than any phantom he could have dreamed up. He shook the thoughts away before he passed the point of no return and frightened her with his curious desire.

She was hurt, though. Scratches marked her hands, knees, and legs, from the rough environment no doubt. The girl was also constantly wetting her lips. They were chapped and red.

I could heal her, give her something to eat, get her to trust me. If she was going to hurt, he was going to be the cause of it; he decided on his next course of action.

"I think you're right, Allie. You can help me. I want you to take me to your transporter ship. I need parts for my flyer and you obviously need supplies," Jack went on, "How about we make a deal?" It was the most rational suggestion he could make and still get the desired outcome.

He could tell the girl thought about it; the proposition of a deal relaxed her, as she had a way out of this alive and unharmed if she was careful. Leading him to the crash wouldn't be as bad as what he really could do to her if he had been a miscreant, a lesser man.

Men he would gladly kill on sight.

Wetting her lips again, "What would I get out of it? How do you know I need supplies?" Knowing full well that he didn't have to offer her anything, that he could kill her and no one would be the wiser.

"You were in my storage unit and based on the way you look, you need something from me. Medicine..." He sniffed, then grimaced to himself, "Soap." A moment passed, "You obviously need these things and I need parts for my ship. You may have noticed by now that I'm not here by choice."

"So," she stammered. "If I take you to my ship, you'll give me these things?" Jack saw the girl's anxiety turn slowly into excitement.

"Yes, I'll supply you, and if you answer my questions along the way, I'll be even more generous. I bet we can learn a thing or two from each other." He really just wanted to crack her open and discover her secrets. Maybe have a little fun while doing it. It didn't matter to him if he had to create the illusion of needing her help if he got something out of it. Not to mention, having a traveling companion would alleviate some of his boredom. He couldn't deny that he was drawn to her.

"I could do that. Would I have to enter the ship? I can lead you there. It would take several days of travel from here but I don't want to enter the place," the girl confessed.

Jack stared at her curiously, "Fine. Don't enter. I don't really care what you do but I won't supply you until we're back here if you're thinking of running off at any point. I don't do search and rescue and I sure as hell don't tolerate deserters. We stick together the whole way, for your safety and for our deal."

"I won't run." She tugged at a strand of her hair in thought. "It's a deal if I don't have to enter."

"Good. Now, why were you trespassing on my ship?" He knew she watched him as he spun the gun around on the table, twirling it into a blurred sphere. She would have viewed it as a threat if he had been looking at her as he played with it but his eyes were fixed on his hand. "Well? Are you going to answer me?" He looked back up at her.

• • • •

DID SHE WANT TO ADMIT that she was here to rob him? No. "I was curious. I wanted to see what was inside." The answer did hold truth to it.

Allie tried to weigh the odds of danger before she accepted his proposal. She didn't entirely trust him. His dark eyes would pin her down one moment and in the next would glaze over; they were unusual and unlike any she had seen before. As long as she only had to take him there but not enter, she would be okay.

The place haunted her nightmares: every day it played with her mind and tried to coax her back. Her heart suddenly felt heavy as if all of this was by design. Maybe this man was sent here to lead her back to the past that she had escaped?

"Why?"

Allie bit her lip and circled her arms around her waist. "I've never seen a ship like this before."

A short silence followed as he looked at her curiously. "How long have you been here?"

"I– I don't know."

She watched as he sighed and ran his hands through his jet-black hair and rose from the chair. All at once her fear came back as he towered over her. She found his presence so intimidating, knowing that he could swat her weak existence out like a bug.

The man came right up to her as if he was going to touch her but stopped short when she had backed up into the cold chrome wall. His arms pinned her on either side of her head caging her in.

"Now unless you want me to throw you in the brig for the rest of the evening, get off my ship." He threatened, his voice masculine and raw. "The day is fading fast and I'm sure you wouldn't want to be caught out here at night."

"You're going to let me go?" She asked incredulously, trying not to focus on how close he was. Allie could stick out her tongue and it would touch the armor plating on his chest.

"Unless you intend to stay, then yes, go." He wanted her to leave. "Come back tomorrow if our deal still stands." He finished.

Allie ducked under his arm quickly without touching him, taking a couple of quick steps away, needing to create some distance. When she turned around to say something more, he was still leaning against the wall but his head was forward and resting on it; his body looked equally tense and rigid but he appeared tired and, choosing to stay silent, she turned and exited the ship.

• • • •

JACK FELT IRRITABLE and oddly content. The girl had finally fallen for his trap and had re-entered his ship, but he couldn't bring himself to watch as she backed away from him to run down the passage, through the hatch, and into the twilight.

Why was she so adamant about not entering the wreckage?

He stayed there against the wall and monitored her progress across the barren landscape until she was safely back in her dwelling. Jack told himself that he didn't care, that it was irrational to care, but he knew that it wasn't the case. He had frightened the girl on purpose but also knew her fear was not because of what he was, a Cyborg, but because she had been caught.

Sighing deeply and pushing away from the wall, he closed the hatch to his ship and retired for the night, choosing to wait out the evening earthquakes in his sleep.

• • • •

ALLIE STILL COULDN'T believe the man had let her leave. The dangerous demeanor and dark eyes he had bored into her as if she were an object to be understood and not a human being, had unnerved her, and had made her skin crawl with an uneasy awareness.

He was unlike the men she had encountered in her previous life and she wasn't sure why. He could have hurt her but had instead had let her leave.

She thought about the bargain they made, wondering if it was worth it. *I need supplies... but do I need them bad enough to trust a stranger?*

Allie ran for a short time until the ship was far enough in the distance that she wouldn't be able to see it if she looked back. She was uneasy about her acquiescence in taking him to the crash site. She had vowed to herself to never return and now she was going to break that vow.

Waiting, watching, and investigating the newcomer had made her create a bond to him that she had never intended to create. She had been alone for so long that this stranger now felt like her closest friend.

Her last friend had died and if she was going to consider this man a friend, she would do what she could to ensure that he stayed alive.

Allie didn't want to show unnecessary weakness in front of the male, but facing her demons and confronting what she had long ago run away from shook her to the core. She was so starved for any company– attention, she realized, that she would actively put herself in jeopardy to prolong the contact.

He would need her to take him to the tomb. She couldn't let a stranger fall prey to the place alone and without warning.

He won't believe me– he already thinks so little of me, she thought as she sat down outside her cave and looked up at the darkening sky, watching the day dissolve away.

• • • •

THE NEXT MORNING ALLIE forced herself to head back to the ship, eating some roots on the walk there, arriving when the sun was at its zenith. When it came into sight, she saw the man outside standing over the area he was repairing, his hand against the metal.

She felt her pulse quicken as she moved closer to him, taking in his large, strangely perfected form. When she was within several yards, he turned and beckoned her into the ship, only stopping when they were back in the center around the circular table.

She watched him disentangle his armor straps, eyeing his weapons and scars. *He's a warrior. I'll be safe with him and he may even scare away the ghosts. Maybe for good.*

She couldn't help but notice how much power he emitted. His presence filled up the room. The man never made any unnecessary movements and his eyes were constantly absorbing everything around him. *I wonder what he thinks of me?* She wanted him to like her. She didn't want another enemy.

I won't let the darkness consume this stranger. Looking at him, sizing him up, she asked, "Have you ever seen a ghost before?" She watched as he sat down and put his elbows on his knees, leaning forward in the process.

"Why? Does your ship have ghosts?" He asked.

"It's filled with darkness. It's why I don't want to enter it."

He laughed. "I'm pretty fucking sure I can get rid of some ghosts for you. I'll even prove to you it's just your imagination," he continued. "They don't exist. There is no known scientific proof of spiritual activity, only hearsay. According to the intergalactic hub," his eyes looked distracted, "ghosts are creations of the living, projections of extreme emotional states, hysteria." He finished, peering at her curiously. "Why do you think there are ghosts in the crash?"

"Can you really prove that they don't exist?" she asked hopefully, taking a step closer to his sitting form. He sat back in his chair and casually looked up at her.

"Sure."

Allie couldn't help the shy smile that appeared on her face.

"We'll leave tomorrow, at sunrise, but for now we'll heal some of those cuts you have while you tell me about this planet."

Relieved, she whispered, "You won't hurt me then? I don't know your name."

He got up abruptly, making her take a step back so as not to collide with him. The man looked at her for a moment before walking away to open a metal panel on the wall. A strange array of medical supplies appeared. He didn't turn back when he answered. "No, I won't hurt you, at least not unless you want me to. Call me Jack. Sit," he demanded, pointing at the table.

Allie chose not to read into his odd statement but instead followed his instructions and went to the table, sitting in the seat he had just vacated.

She looked around nervously at all the foreign, shiny objects the room held. The interior of his ship was pristine yet menacing. There was a soft blue illumination along the pathways and along the walls were the same red strips of light the exterior of the ship had. It was colorful, beautiful yet intimidating. Like it wasn't meant to be appreciated. It was clean, forbidding, and severe.

The crisp neon lighting let her see down the corridor through which she had entered. The hatch was still open but it didn't stop her from feeling trapped.

She turned her attention back to Jack and it was then that she noticed a series of number tattoos across his right upper back where his mesh under armor gapped; a single scar running through them. Suddenly realizing, "You– you're a Cyborg?"

Gasping, "You were in the war. I knew you weren't Earthian, you are much too large but didn't look like a Trent." Her eyes widened. "It makes sense."

• • • •

JACK WAS PREPARING a balm for her chapped lips when she figured out what he was.

"Took you long enough, didn't think you even knew what a Cyborg was. Yes, I'm a Cyborg. I was bred in a vat of nanoparticles and humanoid genes." He turned toward her. "Does that bother you? That I could kill you in a thousand different ways as we speak."

He walked back to the table, placing the fresh salve between them, and coated his middle and index finger. He was momentarily taken aback by her wide bottomless eyes and moved closer.

I touched her earlier. I wonder how long it has been since she's been with another human, let alone a man. He wasn't sure if he wanted to know the answer.

"I don't understand. Why would you be here, a Cyborg? There is no war here..." She hesitated, "Or anyone for that matter."

He smirked at her assumption, "Maybe I'm here to find myself a pretty girl." Liking how she blushed at his comment. *Red would really suit her.* "Now don't move. I'm going to apply this salve I have here to your lips and then to your scratches. It won't hurt but it will tingle." He continued, "There are tiny micro-organisms in it that can replicate and promote new cell growth. I have also mixed in some of my nanocells so I may read your internal system." Staring at her, "Do you understand? They won't be able to affect you in any way. In fact, your body will quickly destroy them but it helps me help you."

While he waited for her to acknowledge, he noticed how intense her stare was and how she began to breath heavier, that her mouth parted slightly. Jack didn't need to scan her to know what kind of reaction she was having to his closeness.

"Yes, I think so."

"Good. It's obvious that you're malnourished, but you may have internal injuries that I'm unaware of." He placed his hand lightly on the back of her neck and the shock of the touch made her surge away from him and away from the table. *Fuck.* He frightened her.

He grabbed her around the waist with his other arm and pushed her back onto the chair.

Allie was struggling against him like a terrified animal. "Stop moving, I won't hurt you. You could have a parasite, or worse, and I will not have you contaminate my ship."

"I'm sorry," she breathed as her struggling slowed down. *Damn, I liked it when she struggled.* When she stopped moving, with his hand still holding her neck, he coated the index and middle finger with his other hand.

"Don't move," Jack warned.

"Okay. I just," she took a deep breath. "This is new to me." He watched her relax.

He breathed in deeply and was immediately engulfed by her pheromones. "Why is this new to you?" He inquired trying to lighten the mood, softly pressing his fingers across her velvety bottom lip.

"It was forbidden to be touched by a male in my colony. I was tested fertile when I turned fourteen cycles, and was placed in a maiden commune, a community of unmated girls and their elders. Infertiles lived there too, in service to us but men were strictly forbidden unless otherwise directed."

Curious he asked, "Earthian colonies don't have a problem with women being fertile. Where were you? You have a Trentian accent."

He could tell she was hesitant about answering him. *What does she think I would do with the information? Take her back?*

"I grew up in a Trentian colony."

"And how did you end up there?" Jack watched her face as she chose her words. Her mouth opening and closing as she decided what to say.

"My mother was Earthian but I never met her. She wasn't born in the colony but belonged to the Warlord's tribe. I don't know how she got there but I know she was pregnant with me before she arrived," she continued, "My mother was smuggled off of her birth colony, I was told, and she was on her way to Xantaeus Trent but she never made it. When she was delivered to the community, along with several other women, she and the others were immediately paired off. When she bore me," she hesitated, "and I was not a half-breed, my mother was cut down by her chosen and I was sent to an orphanage."

As she spoke, he continued to massage her lips back and forth, watching her watch him back. Jack wasn't too pleased with the story, temporarily caring about Pirate Captain Larik's profession and the reasons the Earthian Council hated him; and why he was contracted to capture him.

"So you have had no contact with a man before now?" He asked, intrigued about her innocence.

"The priests–doctors who tested me were men, and that was the first time I was touched by one." She shivered. "It was against the laws of the current Warlord for a maiden to be touched and it was a death sentence for any unworthy male who did. Only the Warlord could honor a male with a female and those males were always the closest to him, the strongest. It was only when he was overthrown by a spurned warrior that I was touched for the second time." She trailed off.

He slowly rubbed the salve over her upper lip, coaxing her body softly with his light touch, watching her eyes go to half mast. His cock was as hard as a rock. *It doesn't help that her body is giving me all the wrong signals,* he thought as he tried to cool off his ardor. *I want her under me but I don't want to frighten her.*

He could smell her desire and was painfully aware that she was pressing her legs together, that the blush hadn't gone away but was deepening.

"It tingles," she whispered.

"Yes, like I said it would." Groaning, he scooped up more of the stuff. "Now open your lips slightly. I'm going to insert some into your mouth. I promise it won't taste like anything." She complied without hesitation and he pushed both fingers in, rubbing her tongue, mimicking the motions like he would if he was fingering her.

Her mouth was hot. And wet. And it drove him crazy.

"Lick the salve off them... make sure you get all of it." He was a goner. *This is so wrong.* The second her mouth closed over his fingers, sucking them while he pushed them further in, he couldn't focus on anything else but her pretty face, his grip on her neck tightened as she moved her tongue all over.

"Fuuck me," he moaned– breaking the trance suddenly– her eyes shooting open. Jack released her and took a step back.

"Did I do something wrong?" she gasped.

"No sweetheart, you were perfect." He backed away, wiping his fingers on his pants. "I think you should apply the rest of the solution yourself. Make sure you get the scrapes on your knees." He needed to remove himself, shut down, and let his cybernetic side take over before he did something he would regret.

• • • •

JACK WALKED OUT OF the room and through one of the corridors, leaving her alone and feeling very confused.

Did I do something wrong? She wanted him to touch her; she had been looking forward to the contact. Realizing that that wasn't going to happen now and feeling oddly rejected, she scooped a dollop of the tingling gel onto her finger and sucked it off.

Hmm, it just isn't the same. At least her lips no longer burned.

She bent over to start rubbing the salve on her cuts when Allie noticed the chair was damp beneath her and her core was throbbing.

Should she find something to clean it up? Looking around, she noticed a cloth at the medical unit Jack had pulled out earlier. Grabbing it, she wiped down the chair then folded the cloth and replaced it where she had found it.

Now that she had cleaned up, she went back to her former task, carefully rubbing the salve over her cuts and scrapes and by the time she was finished, she felt remarkably better, enjoying the healing sensations playing over her skin.

Jack still hadn't come back out so maybe this was his way of dismissing her. Unsure of herself, she called out his name, "Jack." She didn't want to leave without thanking him but when he didn't answer she took that as her cue to leave.

Picking up the little capsule of solution that was left over, she capped it and placed it into her pouch. She was on her way out when his voice rang out behind her.

"Allie," his pitch lowering, sounding rough and incredibly deep. She shivered and saw her freedom vanish as she listened to his steps catch up to where she stood, unmoving.

"We leave at first light tomorrow. If you run then I'll assume the deal is off, find you, and demand payment for the medicine." He was going to let her leave and she found herself thinking she didn't want him to let her leave. "Take this with you." He handed her a small metal disk. It had a thin line of blue light essence along the sides with small ridges along the middle. "If you need me, swipe the sides and call my name."

Without another word and with the disk in her hand– she ran outside and didn't stop until she was curled up in her cave, alone, allowing the soothing, healing sensations to take over.

Chapter Six:

· · · ·

Jack replayed her face sucking his fingers over and over in his mind. She was so innocent and so erotic and in that moment, right before her eyes went wide, he wanted to take her – knowing the repercussions in doing so, he had quickly created some distance.

He was relieved that she left, knowing it was safer this way because playing the hero to a wild girl was just not his fate. Once he checked this transporter ship for pieces, he would patch up his flyer and leave.

It was mid evening now. The girl had left several hours ago and since then he had run the purifiers several times, choosing to erase her presence.

He went about packing supplies for the journey to come. Opening his survival pack he tossed in simple first aid bandages and disinfectants, cleaning fabric for hygiene and ropes, tools, and other such necessities. He chose to only bring two guns with him, a .44 pistol and an assault rifle. Jack didn't expect to run into anything but if there was no shelter to be had at night, he wanted to be prepared.

Jack didn't expect the girl to have much, so he added extra food and water rations to his load.

He looked around, walking through his quarters, and realized he couldn't remember a time when he had to provide for someone else. He had barely met the girl a day ago and he already felt responsible for her safety.

Cyborgs were only responsible to their alliance, themselves, and to other Cyborgs. Even now he knew he could not leave this planet without the girl in tow. It would be cruel to abandon her to this planet alone even if she wanted to stay.

What did my curiosity get me into now?

Walking over to his ship's replicator with a bundle of military grade mesh in his hand, he threw the material in and set it to reconfigure into a small cloak for the girl. The mesh would be breathable during the day and would morph into a well-insulated heat pocket during the night. It wasn't much but it would help keep her warm at night.

He placed the material into his pack, settling into the quiet of his ship.

• • • •

ALLIE HADN'T SLEPT well, lost in a whirlpool of thoughts and not willing to risk sleeping in, she tried to stay up through the night. She didn't want Jack to be mad at her but her half dazed thoughts no longer mattered when a strong voice called her name jerking her out of her half-sleep.

Sitting up she rubbed her eyes, trying to remove the traces of her waking dreams. She slowly focused on the shadow before her blocking out the oncoming dawn.

"I said sunrise. Did you not listen?" The shadow growled.

He's in my cave! How did he find me? And it isn't even sunrise yet!

Glancing at the dim light behind him, she could tell the sun had yet to crest. She appealed, "The sun isn't out yet. I did listen to you, please don't be mad," she stammered. "I can't travel well in the darkness." Even his shadow was imposing, causing a shiver to run up her spine, reminding her of ancient horrors.

"You apparently don't travel well at all," he crouched before her. "Get dressed. We won't be burning daylight for you–what with the monsters at night." He threaded his fingers through her unkempt hair.

"I'm ready to leave. I just need a moment." She disentangled herself from his hand at the same time he stood up.

Allie grabbed her pouch and filled it with roots. *For strength*. She told herself.

He watched her as she moved to the spring and wiped herself down. She rinsed her feet in the cool pool before tying her wrappings around them, and when she was finished she turned around to face him and tried to hide her nerves. "Thank you," she quipped.

She couldn't help but notice he had prepared more for this journey than her. He was in full body armor again, with the black metal and grey mesh, but now he had a large bag strapped to his back and several guns within reach, and he carried the load as if it weighed nothing.

Allie blushed as he just continued to stare at her, feeling a tension thicken the air around them.

· · · ·

JACK WAS INCREDULOUS, "That's it? That's all you're bringing... I thought this was a several day journey, not a casual outing."

She looked around self-consciously. "I don't have anything else," she said before walking over to where she had awoken just minutes ago and picked up her blanket. "I can bring this but it's frayed. It may fall apart. I don't need much out there."

He grabbed the rag from her grasp and tossed it back on the floor. "I have extras. Let's go," he said, climbing out.

She lived in a hole in the ground with barely any tools and a meager food supply. *The only thing going for that rat's nest was the spring. At least she had a source of water and heat.*

He was furious. *Why hadn't she taken more from her crashed ship? Has she really been here that long, that everything was gone?*

Jack grasped her hand as she emerged from the hovel, helping her through the rocky entrance. He noticed, glumly, that she had her blanket under one arm. *She's a proud one.*

Standing up before him, "Please don't throw my things. Like I said, I don't need much to survive on 'HIS,' but everything I do have is precious. I've made this journey before with less."

Choosing not to respond to her comment, he let her take the lead.

They walked the next several miles in silence. *And in the wrong direction.* Jack bristled. He was monitoring their location constantly. *Was she really that upset about the blanket?*

"Is this the right direction?" He inquired slowly, wondering if she was going to try and lead him into a trap.

"Yes..." She looked back at him. "There is a shortcut a half day's walk this way. The crash is on the other side of that mountain bend in the distance," she pointed. "If we scout around the crags this way, we'll eventually come to a tunnel that allows us to cut through the worst of it. It's easier than climbing rocks all day."

"Hmm, if you're sure." Jack scanned the route ahead, sensing no change in structure, no shortcuts.

"The tunnel is burrowed through a rockier route. A giant wurm must have gotten stuck there at one point, long ago. It's held up by its bones."

"Lovely. What can you tell me about them? The wurms that is," he inquired.

She thought for a moment, rounding a large boulder in their way. "They only ever come out at night. I don't think they like the sunlight or the heat. So far I have never gotten close to one, they leave me alone in my cave and they're easy to avoid but I also don't go out at night. Everything changes at night."

"I've noticed the tremors get worse after dark. My readings have confirmed that they are sensitive to UV rays."

Nodding, she continued, "Sometimes they come above ground to fight. They also eat each other sometimes and they spawn thousands of wurms that nest right below the surface. When those wurms die above ground, they provide me a source of food."

Jack grimaced, remembering her meager supply. "I noticed. I saw a pile of bugs in your cave." He paused. "What do you eat out here?" He glanced at her small frame. *She's willing to eat bugs to survive.* He admired that.

"The wurms when I can find them." Allie stopped briefly to look at him. "There are also other little bugs that survive here and some roots if you know where to look for them." She pulled out some to show him. "They grow near the mountains."

He stopped to look at them outstretched in her hand. *The roots had a good source of nutrients and minerals.* He was pleased that she had something else to nourish her besides grubs.

"With a planet infested, literally, with wurms, it's a wonder even these can grow here." He watched Allie eat the roots as they started walking again; Jack stayed by her side.

He looked at her small frame next to him and wondered if she was hungry. Not the daily hunger every person feels, but the type of hunger that occurs after being deprived of food for a significant amount of time.

"Do you want some?" She pulled out more to offer him.

Taken aback by her generosity he replied, "No, thank you. Cyborgs don't eat roots." She continued to look at him for a moment before putting them back into her pouch.

Though Jack could have eaten the roots, they would have done little for his system so he wasn't entirely lying. Cyborgs had far more complicated digestive systems than a human being or Trentian.

His human body needed sustenance, but only a small amount and not very often. He kept protein bars and moleculars on board his ship for just that reason. He had eaten a bar yesterday but only because he transferred a substantial amount of his nanobots to his ship, and creating more took a toll on both his halves.

Jack, like all Cyborgs, had to monitor and maintain his biological side as well as his tech core and processing systems. On one hand, he fed his tech side with updates to his systems. Staying technologically ahead meant constant maintenance to improve speed, cyber reach, and physical endurance.

Cyborgs had a secret central hub that only they had access to, where information was constantly shared. They all fed into it, protected it, and helped maintain it, and he received most of his enhancements from it.

His nanobots erased any damage to his systems, whether technical or physical as they were perfectly attuned to both sides. If one side died then the rest would die too; yes, his consciousness could live on forever as part of the network but he would have no *body* for it. Not unless someone was willing to spend millions of dollars to rebuild him.

• • • •

THEY HAD BEEN WALKING for what seemed like hours, and she had watched the sun's position above out of boredom. It had been mostly silent since their earlier conversation and she hated it. Allie had so many questions that she wanted to ask.

She knew that he had access to information she had only dreamed of but it wasn't really that, she admitted to herself. She wanted to become his friend: make a connection with another being even if it was only for a short time.

A battle raged within herself. On one hand, she desperately wanted to get to know him, but on the other... she was also incredibly intimidated. So after much contemplation, she sadly resolved to stay quiet and only sneak glances in his direction.

Allie liked how he looked and she found herself appreciating him in full survival mode. *Jack.* She thought to herself that he could probably kill the Warlord and all his Generals without hesitation.

Glancing over again– he still looked so stern, so fierce, with his short dark hair catching strays of light that gave it a fleeting indigo gleam. Her former captors were no match for him, she fantasized, imagining he was there that day she stood in line with the other terrified girls.

The Warlord would have just arrived and before he even touched the first girl, Jack would appear out of nowhere and gut him from behind. She pictured him with his dagger in hand and the blood of the Warlord dripping down its sharp edge.

That he would look up and meet her eyes.

That he would walk over to her with purpose.

That he would–

It was a nice fantasy, but that was all it was.

Finally, she felt the courage to break the silence, "Why are you here–errr–I mean what brought you close to this planet?" she asked cautiously.

He looked her way. "I'm hunting."

That was ominous. Confused she asked, "Hunting for what?"

"A man."

"But there is no one here but me." *Was there somebody else?*

He looked over at her but said nothing.

The conversation dropped and another hour went by. The sun was directly above them before the silence broke again.

• • • •

"LET'S REST HERE. YOU can eat while I look around." Jack dropped his pack on a nearby rock, opening it.

"I don't need to rest and I ate earlier," she said.

Jack just stared at her, assuming she was referring to the handful of roots; he ignored her comment. He pulled out a protein ration and handed it to her.

"Take this and eat it. It'll give you strength. I hope you like vanilla." He snickered at his joke.

She looked at him again. *If she continues to give me those doe eyes, I'm going to push her to the ground and take her right here.* In the dirt, in broad daylight, and in the middle of this wasteland.

"I've never had vanilla before." Taking the ration reluctantly when he unwrapped it, she nibbled the edge and moaned.

His shaft went hard at the sound. He watched with fascination as her lips puckered around the oblong bar to nip a piece off, and he had to forcefully hold back a groan as her throat contracted and swallowed it down. Who knew watching someone eat could be such a turn on?

I want to feel that throat contract around my cock.

She murmured a thanks as he quickly walked off to scout around. Jack wasn't sure what intrigued him so much about her. The fact that she smelled like a mixture of sweat and sex, or the fact that she was so beautiful and vulnerable– or maybe it was his processor's malfunctioning. His human half seeing something in her that he thought he would never have.

He scaled a ledge to scan the horizon, his thoughts coming to an abrupt halt; a monstrous skeletal forest was coming into view.

It was a forest of dead wurms. Their skeletons towered up from the ground to look like decrepit pale-white trees. He'd seen battlefields more cheerful than this. Unnerved, he settled down to stare at the scene before him.

The forest of bone extended out for miles with no end in sight, only coming to a stop at the base of the mountain. Did the creatures come here to die? Or did they hit the rocks and splatter against them?

He could feel a deep rumble and shift below the rocky surface, miles beneath him, as the beasts moved. It lulled him into a strange sense of calm, being at the edge of an endless graveyard of monsters and feeling the weak vibrations below him. Everything was dead–quiet–as far as the eye could see.

Some of his brethren had found women over the years preceding the war. Yuric, his commander, was the only one to take a mate during the war and they all thought him a lunatic at the time, having to protect his woman and fight a war at the same time. Now he remembered with envy.

It was rare when a Cyborg mated with a woman, as there were a lot of risks involved. They were created with the intention to inflict violence, to do jobs and fight battles that human men could not. Cyborgs could restrict their humanity when needed. Although none of his mated brethren had ever hurt their women, not one union had failed and children had been fostered, there was still always that risk.

Not to mention it was difficult to find a woman in the galaxies, as their sex vastly changed their rarity, status, and power in each sector.

The expansions that were pushed and made by the intergalactic council to travel out to deep space had thinned out the populations so much that it was hard to pinpoint an exact number or even estimate how many people there were.

Women weren't rare exactly, but they were well protected by Earthians and even more so by the Trentians.

It didn't matter whether they were Trentian, Earthian, or half-breed, the Trentians were fanatically obsessive in their protection. And what kind of woman would want a Cyborg? Especially since it was widely believed that they were more robots than men, that they were violent and unpredictable, and that they couldn't procreate.

It was because of that mindset and that risk that Jack didn't know if he could trust himself with a female, especially with the burden of taking one in union. He had been with women before but had never bonded intimately. His logical side saw no reason for it but now his logistics were strangely silent.

Jack stood up, sparing one last glance at the boneyard and started to walk back toward the girl. Maybe he was viewing her like one of his missions... and he never failed a mission.

He spied on her before making his presence known. She was stuffing a small part of the protein ration into her pouch that carried her roots and other supplies. He smiled to himself.

She was looking around, probably for him, before staring absently at her hands deep in thought.

I hope she's thinking about me.

"Let's get going," he grunted, coming into view. She scurried up at the prompt and they continued on.

They walked in silence for the rest of the day.

He had been surprised that she was correct with regard to the shortcut. At first, he had been wary of the rocky, skeletal tunnel but he had sensed no wurm activity nearby. He placed his hand on what appeared to be a rib bone of the giant dead wurm to read the structure and came away with a powdery white calcite substance all over his hand. *Well, it's strong enough to hold up this tunnel,* he thought as he wiped his hands until the crystals fell away.

After his assessment, they continued on.

The daylight faded rapidly and the temperature began to drop as the sun headed for the horizon.

Jack led them to a large outcropping of rocks and found them a nook between several boulders. It wasn't the most comfortable location but it would provide some protection, and he set about lighting a fire. There was no kindling to be had, so he created an oil based flame and lit it with an electrical current.

"This won't last us the whole night, but it will keep us warm for now," he said as the girl stared at the flame, probably determining whether it was safe. "It's been a long time since you've seen a flame," he stated rather than asked.

"Yes. The last time was during the aftermath of the crash when the ship was in flames." She settled in, pulling her blanket around her, appreciating the warmth. The evening descended into darkness around them, the only source of light coming from the fire and the subtle moonbeams outside.

They were undisturbed except for faint tremors now and again.

• • • •

ALLIE MOVED CLOSER to the fire – *I'm so cold.*

A silence had fallen between them again. It didn't help that Jack was sharpening his dagger tensely, exacerbating the poignant feeling in the air. She decided to focus on the fire and staying warm, only stealing glances his way.

"Is there something on my face?" He grinned, putting his weapon away. "You've been watching me all day," he goaded her.

"It's not every day a male comes into my life," she said, annoyed.

"Do they come in often?" With a teasing note to his voice, he continued to grin at her.

Allie sighed, "Not in a very, very long time."

Jack's tone became serious, amping up the tense atmosphere between them again. "You mentioned earlier you had been touched during your fertility testing. The next time... was it an admirer? Consensual?"

"The next time is why I'm here."

He glared at her, she could tell he was willing her to continue. *He's very demanding.*

"What happened that was so bad you ended up stranded on a planet billions of miles from anyone, anywhere, alone?" His voice lowered with dark authority. She felt she had no choice but to obey him.

Moving closer to the fire between them, she began. "Where I'm from fertile females are very rare. We're prized and protected, living in a community away from everyone else. The commune I was kept in was run by elders, barren females, and militarized drones. Men were strictly forbidden to enter unless they were there to choose a bride– gifted by the Warlord," she continued. "There was a man, shamed, not given a bride– who eventually killed the Warlord and took over the colony. The new Warlord and his Generals, other men who had also held the grudge of being spurned, came to our commune and hurt us."

• • • •

"ALLIE." JACK STABBED his dagger into the ground. "What's this place called?" He needed her to tell him, knowing the horrors that would have been committed, sickened by this unknown man.

"Kreatiax was the name of the port town near where the other girls and I were kept, but we only knew our home as the colony. It had no real name to us," she murmured.

Jack logged all data into his hard drive unit to research later. He would have to find this place and make a side trip there. Or maybe give this information over to the Earthian council. Either way, it would be dealt with. *Maybe this information can help me find Larik.*

Allie was shivering. He watched as she moved dangerously close to the flame.

"Here, I made you something to keep you warm." He pulled out the black mesh material from his pack.

"You made me something?" She stared at him in wonder.

"I told you I would supply you," he declared angrily. "You're practically naked in those rags you wear. The cloak will help shield you from the elements," he said as he draped it around her shoulders, regretting that he had not given it to her earlier.

"This is... very nice, Jack." She gasped, running her fingers along the fabric. "Thank you."

"Now continue with your story," he demanded, wishing he had brought her more, feeling a protective urge travel through his systems. He wanted to be the one to keep her warm, irrationally envious of the cloak around her shoulders. *I can heat my body up with electricity and she would never have to be cold again if she stayed in my arms.*

And he could tell she didn't want to continue, didn't want to let him into her past. But his eyes gave her little option but to finish telling him. He knew he had the look of someone who often got what they wanted. She breathed, defeated. "Soon after the rebellion, the men came and announced that all maidens of age would be presented to him," she shook her head. "One by one he violated us all, checking for our innocence and then taking it away." She stared blankly. "No girl was pure by the end and his Generals did worse once he chose a bride amongst us."

Jack felt murderous and knew he had that look about him now, swiping his dagger back and forth across his palm. "Did they rape you?" Disgusted by the primitive, savage men. They had no right to a female– let alone this female.

He decided.

After his mission, he would find this colony and wash it away in blood.

"Not me. I wasn't raped, I was the Usurper Warlord's chosen. I was to undergo a ritual but some of the other girls..." she trailed off.

"Did this Warlord rape you during this ritual?" He could envision his blood soaking his hands. His processors were now on overdrive, collecting any and all information about this colony. Kreatiax was a port on a backwater Trentian planet that could sustain a vast ecosystem but was so far away from normal hubs it was often left alone.

"He never had the chance to. We escaped– those of us who could– ran that night to the port. We boarded a transporter ship and escaped. We ran because we were frightened, hoping for a brighter future." She whispered. "One that didn't last very long."

"Then you crashed here?"

"Yes. The ship malfunctioned, randomly, suddenly and it crashed into a mountain, a day and a half from here." He watched as she noticeably began to tire and droop toward the ground. "I was the only survivor."

"Come here, Allie." He reached out his hand to her.

She looked at it suspiciously before taking it. He moved her next to him and put his arms around her small frame. *Let me keep you warm.* Her body was tense against him and it made him sad.

"I won't hurt you. I'm not like those other men. When I touch a woman, she's begging for it, not crying," Jack said. "I'm going to keep you warm tonight and prove to you that not everything that happens between a man and a woman is bad." Allie rolled around to face him while his arm grasped her body flush against him, letting his warmth penetrate her as he heated up.

"I feel safe with you. I don't know you, but I feel safe with you," she breathed, to the man who was still a stranger. "If you were going to hurt me, you would have done it by now."

Jack tightened his arms around her and buried his face into her hair.

Chapter Seven:

• • • •

It was a short while later before Allie was asleep in his arms. Jack wanted her badly. He wanted to infect her body with himself and ravage her system. *I want to grind her into the ground and pound into her tight sheath.* He felt like he was malfunctioning because his systems were having vitriolic reactions to the situation. His humanity felt quietly happy; nothing about him was in accord anymore.

Everything that he said to her was the truth but it felt like a lie. His violence extended beyond himself and for some reason, he had tunnel vision with her – the moment his ship had landed a week ago. That tunnel vision only grew worse the more time he spent in her presence. If the Warlord and his men were still alive, he would make sure it wouldn't be for long.

He just had to take it slow but he couldn't deny that he would have her. Thinking this to himself, he fell into a frustrated, dreamless sleep.

Jack's eyes snapped open. Something was wrong. The fire was fading now, its glow only casting small shadows around them.

He quietly unsheathed his dagger, trying hard not to disturb the sleeping girl in his arms. He went on full alert, every muscle in his body tensed with anticipation.

It started out as a rumble, the pebbles around their forms scattering about, vibrating in sync with the ground beneath them. There was something just below their location and approaching very fast.

"Allie," he nudged. "We need to move." She sat up slowly with his help, rubbing the sleep from her eyes.

"What's happening?" She whispered, looking around before she registered the shaking beneath her feet. She shot up from the ground, panic filling her eyes.

"There are several giant creatures moving this way – Fast!" Jack grabbed her around the waist, slinging his pack behind his back at the same time. He dragged them out of the small cave and away.

The tremors were earth-rendering shakes. The rocks dislodged from their positions in the dirt from the violent vibrations. Jack, without letting go of Allie, weaved between the craggy terrain and away from the danger, ascending to higher, rockier ground. The giant stone monoliths fell away as a behemoth broke through the surface, shooting up into the sky with a deafening roar where they had been moments before.

Allie turned around at the noise, gasping, as the ground they were just sleeping on opened up into a jagged scar. The spiky back of a sand serpent moved directly through the tear it had created.

There were two beasts behind them now, clashing into each other, making the rocky crags their own personal battle arena. One dove back into the dirt as the other, covered in saw-like scythes, slithered around in a circular pattern. Jack turned back frequently to monitor them but it quickly appeared that the beasts were not in pursuit. It was the crashing, wanton destruction around them that posed the most threat.

He weaved up and around the bedrock, only stopping to help Allie through the trickier parts, knowing her sight was not as good as his in the dark. The wurms behind them were weaving in and out, quickly making their battle arena into a large death pit.

"What's happening?" she asked, trying to catch her breath.

Jack pulled her along, trying to create more distance. He really didn't want them to be sucked down into the wurm's personal quarry, smashed to. He could take down one bug, he knew, but he was unsure of his ability to take down two while still worrying about the girl's safety. He also didn't think his assault rifle and pistol would do more than annoy the creatures, anyway.

"It may be a territory dispute. There must be hatchlings nearby and our presence may have been felt – may have aggravated them." He stopped briefly, putting the knife he still had in his hand away. He touched his eye, triggering his infrared vision.

"They've never bothered me before," she said, when a wurm, still dangerously close emerged from the ground only to dive back into the pit. The creatures could block out the stars.

Jack gripped her arm again, "We need to keep moving, we need more distance between us and them. I think they may be drawing more friends."

They trekked through the shaking landscape, sometimes stopping as it brought them to their knees. Jack slowed at times to let Allie catch her breath and to watch the interaction behind him. It was a incredible sight: complete and utter destruction was always a thing to behold. It called to him at a spiritual level.

His blood was pumping, his adrenaline coursing through his system, making him restless and ready for action. He either wanted to jump into the fray and get his hands dirty or take out his frustration on the female next to him. He wouldn't risk her life though, or the fragile trust that had begun to build between them. He also glumly had to remind himself that he left his long-range carbine laser back at the ship.

He and Allie had been moving steadily up the mountainside for the past hour. She hadn't said anything since the action. Looking her way, her face looked pensive and tired. They couldn't keep this up without bringing more attention to themselves.

The night was still young and she needed more rest. "Let's stop here." Settling his pack on the ground.

"Thank you." She breathed heavily, "Thank you for saving our lives."

He murmured a reply to her while he unloaded a blanket.

"Do you think it may have been the fire that brought them? I've never drawn them to me before like that. Maybe they could feel the heat?"

"I'm not so sure. They do have an incredible sensory system. It may be me that they are after. I have a lot of alien devices that are part of me that could distress them, and I was stressing my systems to keep you warm." Jack watched the wurms crisscrossing around each other from his vantage point. "Our presence is small. There may be a nest nearby but once again, we posed no threat to it." He smirked. He watched as the wurms were up to something entirely different now.

Laughing, "It looks like our pet monsters are breeding."

Allie looked at him quizzically. "It would make sense if we were close to a nest."

• • • •

THERE WAS AN AWKWARD silence that followed as the adrenaline from the run wore off. Allie sat down with her new cloak pulled tightly around her, feeling the chill creep back into her bones. She had felt safe and warm in his arms while they rested earlier. She was silently cursing the wurms to Hell for disturbing them because now she was cold again, missing his presence like a scorch to her skin.

She couldn't see what Jack was focused on but she could hear the roars of the beasts behind them and feel the shakes beneath her.

"Well this is interesting, our male wurm has quite some prowess," Jack said with amusement.

"What's happening between them?" Allie asked. Jack snapped his eyes away from the scene and focused on her. His attention was solely on her again – she wasn't sure if she liked it or if she should be afraid. But it was what he did next that surprised her.

"How about you see for yourself?" He reached into a side pocket on his survival pack and pulled out a disk, not unlike the one he gave her before. She watched in curiosity as a screen projected up from the middle of it. "Come here," he demanded gruffly.

Without hesitation this time, she moved over to him as he sat down on the rocky ledge, resting his back against the mountain wall. When she got close enough to his lounging position, he gripped his hands over her hips and set her between his legs, wrapping an arm around her middle. She couldn't be sure if it was to keep her still or to keep her warm or both, but she felt cocooned and safe again.

Jack handed her the disk with the holographic screen. "Hold this up and look through it. The screen is in infrared so although you won't be able to make out exact details, you should be able to see the wurms."

She moved the screen so she was now holding it up with both hands, leveling it with her eyes, and looked into it. Allie gasped at the scene playing out before her; seeing the beasts at night was something she had never experienced before. They were so large they could eclipse the sun.

It unnerved her that these giants roamed below her at night and she was suddenly, incredibly thankful they had never decided to fight or mate where her cave was. She would have been a blip to them, a particle of sand, so insignificant they would have never known she was there.

I think I may move into the mountains after this trip is over.

"If you look closely, you'll notice that there are three bugs out there now. It appears our male is a stud and has attracted more than one admirer," Jack continued, absently playing with her hair. "The females are fighting each other for breeding rights. I have a feeling they're going to have a long night ahead of them... I don't know if I should feel envious of the male."

"How do you know it's not two males fighting over a female?" She asked, watching the wurms through her screen.

"Mmm, well, my scans indicate that two of them are in heat with unfertilized eggs. The third one is not." He pulled her hair away from her and draped it across one shoulder, leaning in.

"Why would you be envious?" The mood between them changed– her question came out as a breath when her attention shifted from the screen to the tugging, relaxing sensations of her hair being played with. His mouth moved back and forth right above her skin.

"Any man would be envious. To have a female want you so bad, she was willing to fight for it." Jack's face nuzzled against the sensitive spot between her neck and shoulder. His breaths grew louder as he seemed to be breathing her in while she herself could barely breathe; feeling him harden against her back. *Does he want me?* Allie could hardly believe it. No man would want a girl like her– dirty and shameful and cursed.

But he doesn't know that I'm cursed.

"Allie... would you fight for it?" He whispered into her neck making goosebumps appear on her skin.

"For a man?" she asked breathlessly.

"Yes," he said. She could feel him reposition himself behind her when his hard-on rubbed across her back.

"He would have to be the right one..."

Her eyes closed as she clutched the screen. His mouth lifted away from her neck at her answer and she felt the loss of his heated lips with disappointment.

"What would make a man... the right one?"

She wondered at his question as she had never really thought about it before. She tried to envision her perfect man but could only see Jack in her mind. *I don't think he would appreciate it if I was honest.* So she decided to describe him instead.

He tugged her hair, waiting for her response.

Allie focused on the wurms through her screen rubbing up against each other. "He would have to be strong and kind."

Jack laughed softly at her answer, his breath tickled her hair. "That's it? There are billions of men in the universe and you just described at least twenty percent of them." His hand cupped her jaw from behind and turned her face toward him. "There has to be more."

With the red light coming from the screen in her hands, she could see her neon self-reflected in his eyes. His pupils glistened with the color and it made them look sharp and demonic.

"He would have to be as strong physically as he is of character." She licked her lips and dropped her gaze, not wanting to fall into it. "He would have eyes that told his story, even if it was a bad one. The right man would be sure of himself – confident. He would want me for me and not for my womb."

Jack's hands began to caress her neck and shoulders as he, in turn, looked away. His eyes glazed over, his expression far away. *I wish I knew what he was thinking.*

"Does it matter if he were Earthian or Trentian?" he asked.

"Or Cyborg," she finished and paused. "I've never met an Earthian male and I have only had negative experiences with Trentian men."

Allie lost her breath as he looked back at her with urgent possession.

"Men from all over the universe would lay down their lives for a chance with you." He whispered into her ear, making her hair stand on end.

Please, want me.

She had no time to answer him when his mouth latched onto her and bit down, his tongue lapped at her skin as if he had read her thoughts.

The bite was hard enough to feel uncomfortable but soft enough not to draw blood. It felt like a branding. The brief scrapping of his teeth sent electric currents jolting to her core, making her aware of how wet she had become and how empty she was beginning to feel.

This wasn't anything like her time alone when all she had were desperate fantasies to take care of her. Jack was real and he was advancing on her.

His other arm tightened around her as he pressed her up against his erection roughly. Like he was trying to fill her emptiness by sheer force of will.

"You smell so damn good," he said as he placed little kisses along her neck while bending his knees closer and pressing himself into her. Allie was awash in foreign sensations.

She was afraid of him, of what he could do, but at the same time, she found herself wildly craving his attention, losing herself in his desire for her. She felt powerful – that this Cyborg warrior was mindlessly groping her, that she could do this to a man.

Maybe she could still join with a man after all that had happened, and everything that she had been through hadn't made her impure. Her elders be damned.

It was then that Jack's hand found her breast underneath the cloak and massaged it. She dropped the screen with a startled moan, placing her hands on his knees for support.

"Oh Allie, I have been smelling your wet heat for days," he groaned as he pulled the cloak away from her chest and tugged the wrap around her breasts off, exposing her. He quickly covered them up with his hands while hooking his feet under her legs, spreading them wide. The only barrier between her and his gaze was the cloth still covering her up between her legs.

"Sweetheart, be a good girl and grab the back of my head and rub that ass against me. Let me prove to you being with a man can be very pleasurable," he demanded, lightly pinching her nipples.

Allie moaned as he anchored her against his armored body.

She could buckle, fight, and scream, knowing he wouldn't let her go. He was giving her a way to lose control within a controlled environment. She felt all the years of pent up frustration start to pour out of her nerve endings. "Jack," a breathy whisper escaped.

His touch was demanding yet gentle and she could barely focus with all the new sensations coursing across her skin and through her body. His breath was hot on her shoulder. His light tugs on her nipples with the insistent grinding of his cock along her lower back captivated her attention and she couldn't be sure if it was herself grinding against him or vice versa.

Did this man really want her? Her insecurity was a constant, looming shadow in her mind. Would he still want her after this moment ended? She warred with herself, the thoughts seizing her, pulling her away from the frustration and as if he could read her, his hand let go of her breast with a desperate squeeze and softly moved over her ribs, over her belly and settled below her pelvis. His fingers were whisper-caresses over her sensitive skin.

His straining muscles that had been trapping her in the cell of his arms loosened their hold around her.

Why was he suddenly slowing down?

Her breath hitched, anxiously wanting to know what he would do next, but his hand didn't move. Instead, his other hand wrapped around her body and held her against him, the onslaught of passion abruptly stopped and faded away.

She had the urge to scream.

"Shhh, girl. I'm not going to hurt you," Jack said as his delicious mouth glided over her neck. "I have wanted you my entire life. I just hadn't realized it until I saw you on my ship," he whispered as the energy between them continued to dissipate and exhaustion took its place.

She could still feel him hard against her and it made the wet, empty longing between her legs ache. Her only consolation was his mouth nuzzled against her neck.

Allie turned her head to look at him, "I liked how you made me feel. Why did you stop?" She had to know if it was something she had done.

He laughed, "If you liked that – and I know you did, you smell like sex and desperation to me – you'll love when I touch you next time." He wrapped the cloak back around her and unpinned her feet. She turned in his arms to face him.

His gaze went directly toward her still exposed breasts. "There will be a next a time?" she asked hopefully.

Staring at her breasts, he responded, "Oh yes. We'll make it part of our deal." He smirked. "Those could kill a man." His hands moved up her sides, his eyes rapt as he cupped them, watching intensely as he stroked one peak with the pad of his thumb.

"I'm not going to take you on the ground, in the middle of this hellish pit, with giant ugly monsters roaring in the background for your first time," he said as he pressed her breasts together, now rubbing both her nipples.

He leaned in and sucked a taut peak into his mouth. She felt the heat pool between her legs again as her head fell back. His mouth was lavishing her tits, sucking them, licking them while still rolling them with his fingertips. She sat forward, right over his erection.

"Damn it, Allie," he said without lifting his mouth away, "you're making this really hard for me."

She giggled, feeling bold. "But you're already hard."

Jack pulled away from her, his expression not amused but instead stern. He crashed his lips against her mouth, kissing her with a roughness that bordered close to pain. She parted her lips from the passionate assault and his tongue penetrated the open barrier.

She heard him groan against her mouth as his hands left her breasts, giving her puckered nipples one last pinch. Jack's hands circled behind her and ran down her exposed back, leaving a burning heat in their path, to have them end up cupping her buttocks.

He lifted her up like she weighed nothing and redirected her legs to straddle his hips, the armor plating on his thighs dug into her legs as she was settled on top of his erection.

She bounced up with a pleasured mew when he lifted his hips off the ground to grind into her. She had to circle her fingers around the weapon's straps across his chest for support.

A gasp escaped her as he lifted his lips away. "I should have started with a kiss," he said as he rubbed his mouth against hers.

"I liked it." She pressed her mouth back against his, softly.

"Was it your first?" His warm hands ran up her body to bury in her hair.

"Yes."

"Good." He smirked as his grip in her hair tightened. Their breath mingled as neither of them moved, unsure of where to go from here. "Allie..." he trailed off.

She leaned back to look at him, his eyes caught hers and what she saw made her nervous: he looked fervid and violent. "Is something wrong?"

He moved a hand from her hair and slid it down, groping her breast before moving it down between her legs as he forced his hand between them. The pressure made her want to scream as the tension reached a crescendo.

"I'm going to take care of you." He took her mouth again. "Do you trust me to take care of you?"

The question startled her as she hadn't thought about it. She sat back and looked into his expectant eyes. *Should I trust him?* It brought reality down around her shoulders. Her tongue felt thick as she strived to answer his question.

She jerked up when the hand between her legs cupped her sex and lifted her. The next thing she knew he was towering over her and the aura of his domineering presence pushed her back into the stone ground.

"I think you want to trust me." Jack trapped her as he whispered the sentiment into her ear. "I think you're aching to trust me." His finger prodded the entrance to her core, pushing the damp fabric into her.

She squirmed as his finger massaged her in slow, agonizing circles.

"What are you going to do?"

"You need to shatter. You need to break apart into a thousand electrifying pieces," he breathed into her ear, making her toes curl. "And then you need to be remade."

• • • •

HE LIFTED AWAY FROM her, snaking down her heated body, trailing her skin with his breath until he was between her tense legs. She was driving him mad with desire. His dick was hard enough to tear through his belted pants.

I want to take her innocence like it was the last thing I would ever do. Jack bit his tongue at the thought. He could hear the roars of the violently mating wurms in the background, he could smell the carnage from the battle the two females wrought, and he could tell that Allie was strummed tighter than a live-wire before him.

When she had answered his question about what her perfect man would be and she had said Cyborg, Jack nearly lost his control. He wanted to harness his reaction and make her feel it like he had. He wanted her to break like he had almost done.

She's going to lose her naive innocence to me. She's going to lose her innocence to a Cyborg. The thought was erotic and wrong in his head as he dug his finger into her pussy. Hard enough to make her shiver but soft enough not to tear the flimsy, damp fabric of her clothing.

"Trust me?" he ground out.

"Y–yes."

"Good girl." He slipped her covering to the side and slid his finger into her.

Her hips flew upward and she shrieked. "Jack!" He laid his other arm across her stomach and pushed her back into the ground. Their eyes caught. He smirked at her uncertain expression as he began to thrum her secret spot.

"Let go, Allie." He pushed a second finger as he kept eye contact with her lust-clouded pupils.

"I can't," she gasped.

"You can."

Her legs bent up and widened around him as she struggled against his fingers. He noticed her nails scratching at the rock on either side as her body tried to retain the tension he was coaxing out.

"I can't, Jack." Her gasp turned into a cry.

"Trust me to pick up the pieces."

The tremors from the mating beasts behind them became tremors of her own at his words. Her body followed his order and convulsed into his hand. Jack lifted his arm off her stomach as she undulated.

"Good girl," he whispered again as he held her and she writhed into him. "It's not smart to tease me."

It was some time before the tension passed. He settled himself next to her and pulled her into his chest. He never once let her go as he ran his fingers back through her disheveled hair and put her back together.

Chapter Eight:

• • • •

Jack held her for the rest of the night. Listening to her breathing, lulling him into a state of calm awareness as the night lightened into dawn. The wurms had ceased their interactions several hours prior.

He was a tornado, a myriad of emotions, none of them easy to weather – or fun to deal with. His life had been straightforward a week ago, revolving around the missions he took up and the reputation he wanted to maintain. He was the best bounty hunter in this galaxy and many galaxies over, and it had always been stiff competition to be so.

Just two days ago, his thoughts were consumed with the capture of Pirate Captain Larik, of turning him in but also of his revenge, which now seemed petty. The pirate was wanted for crimes against humanity, against Earthians, and most of all against women. At least that was what the council argued.

Jack knew that Larik only transported willing women, women who wanted a different life, women who specifically sought him out. It made him wonder about the man who had piloted the crashed transporter that Allie had been on many years ago.

What were his reasons for helping the fleeing females from their fate? He knew he would never know, but boy did he love to speculate.

The sun was beginning to crest but he was still lost in thought. Thoughts were like light and shadow, sunrise and sunset, always there, always eternal but fleeting. Yet his thoughts had yet to desist.

He was a Cyborg. A bounty hunter. A hardened warrior created for a war that was not his own. Could he also be more? His logic fell uncomfortably silent with the question.

The one thing he did know for certain was that he wanted to be off this planet. Whether it was with Allie or not, he was still unsure. He knew he couldn't leave her here, not anymore. Not even if she begged.

That fate would have been cruel especially when the universe held so much more. He was convinced that his strange need for her would come to an end, as all things did. That the insanity that had set in his mind would dissipate.

Once he felt in control again and this situation became part of his past.

Jack would get the parts he needed for his ship and he would keep his end of the bargain. He would also collect his bounty for Larik's capture and then he would move on. He thought all of this as he looked down at the sleeping girl in his arms, giving her a small squeeze.

He would take care of her as well.

"Allie, wake up." He gently squeezed her again as the sun detached itself from the horizon. She shifted in his arms at the prompt.

He watched as her mind and body slowly awoke before his eyes. The rays of the sun hitting her skin made her glow like an ethereal jewel. He could sense her heart rate gradually increase as her awareness returned.

Jack shifted upward as she pulled herself away from his chest and into a sitting position. Her fingers grasped the cloak over her breasts.

"Good morning, Allie."

She looked at him with wide eyes. He watched as she replayed what had transpired between them last night.

"Jack," she said warily, sitting further back, creating more distance between them.

"I meant what I said last night." He stared at her, waiting for her next move. She seemed to either be at a loss for words or thinking about her response.

After several more moments passed she said, "I meant it too." The tension growing thick again with her response, his smile growing wider. Not only was his wild girl proud but she was also bold.

He casually got up, feeling great all of the sudden. He reached down to pick up her top that he pulled off her last night and reluctantly handed it over.

"I would prefer that you remain topless but since I'm such a gentleman, I'll let you decide." Jack watched, amused as she snatched her top away and tied it on under her cloak.

She got up and rubbed the dirt off her skin. Realizing that she didn't have any supplies with her but her food, he pulled out a nano-cybotic cleaning cloth from his pack and handed it to her. "Wipe this over your skin. It will clean you better than soap and water. It just won't feel as good."

"Thank you." She blushed, taking it from him. He turned to give her some privacy as she bent down to clean herself up. He strapped his weapons on instead and secured the pack to his back– ready to start the day.

When she was done, he took the cloth back, while she shyly grabbed his hand and led him away.

Jack looked down at their joined hands. The connection was innocent but it burned a path as fast and as hot as wildfire to his robotic heart. He pushed the odd feeling away and disengaged himself.

They were back on their way toward the shipwreck just as dawn transformed to day.

The morning passed by in a companionable silence, the tension that lingered between them from the previous day gone for now. The sun had ascended above, raising the temperature to an uncomfortable itch. It wasn't long before Allie shook off the cloak. He took it from her without a word and bundled it into his pack.

The crags slowly turned into the base of the mountain, the jagged rocks now more of a dip into large, rocky valleys. The trek became more of an upward crawl, climbing out of pits.

At several points, he had to take out his rope and help her over the worst of the ledges. He didn't need help himself, scaling the escarpment without a thought but always wary of his companion's fragility.

She had no armor, no protection, but he could tell that she was used to the inhospitable environment. She never flinched when landing hard on her feet or gaining another unintended scratch. It was over the course of the morning that he noticed that she sported tiny, faded scars over her delicate skin, not unlike his own.

She's not afraid of pain. It was probably a common occurrence in her life.

Good thing he had everything he would need to heal her wounds.

They remained along the base of the mountain, following it as a guide. Jack knew that they were closing in on their destination; the dead structure became a prominent fixture in his mind as he surveyed their location. It was larger than he had originally thought but his most recent readings had been consistently muddied. It seemed that the closer they came to it, the harder it was for him to focus on it.

He didn't like it but he could attribute it to an unknown technology or mechanical structure – maybe radiation. Whatever it was, he logged his readings on his personal hard drive to upload later to the central hub for research. Other Cyborgs may know why he was having such difficulties with it.

At the pace he and Allie had been traveling, they wouldn't arrive at their destination until after dark. He could have been there already and gone if it was just himself but that would have put a kink into his other, more personal mission. He turned his eyes to look at her.

She wasn't much of a talker but still... she hadn't spoken in hours, and she must be getting hungry. Just as he was going to suggest taking a break, she reached into her threadbare pouch at her waist and pulled out roots to chew on, eating them while she walked.

He waited and willed her to suggest taking a break but she just kept walking.

Jack let her take the lead as he stewed. *She barely speaks and isn't making any move to stop and rest.* How was he going to gain her trust if he couldn't even talk to her? Being friendly and conversational were qualities that he did not have.

If she could just pretend– for five minutes– that she needed him desperately, to save her from this place, to supply her
protection, or even just wanted to *talk* to him, he could
progress his side mission. But no, she kept walking forward in
grim silence as if every step led her to an unwanted, inevitable
end.

Her thoughts were elsewhere and he didn't like it.

• • • •

THE DAY HAD STARTED off nicely. Allie woke up warm
and relaxed in Jack's arms. She still couldn't believe what had
transpired between them the night before, and she only hoped
that they would have the chance to touch each other like that
again.

But the morning had faded and so had her good mood. The
once comfortable silence now felt like a void, making her ears
want to pop under the pressure.

She knew why she felt this way – she always did the closer
she got to her past. But she had hoped that having a warrior,
like the Cyborg next to her, would embolden her resolve
enough to face what was ahead with courage. *It's not working.*

Every step felt like she was descending further into her own
personal Hell. Glancing at the man next to her, she could tell
that his mood wasn't holding up either.

It was always like this. She could tell him but she was smart
enough to know that he would find her warnings ridiculous,
unbelievable. Anyone would have who had never seen the
darkness like she had, and not just any darkness, like the natural
absence of light, but a deeper, terrible darkness not of this
world.

That darkness was a part of her now and she tried to keep it buried deep – hiding it from herself and from the world. It fed off of her guilt and her shame... and sometimes, when the tremors stopped at night when her fears became thick, it would seep into her cave, her thoughts, and tugged at her soul.

She had seen the darkness snuff out the light around her until she was trapped in an endless abyss, the heavy press of it crushing her. At the worst moments, she could hear distant screams, quiet cries sneaking up behind her.

But it never lasted. It would vanish as quickly as it had appeared. Allie wasn't sure it was just her sanity becoming unhinged or a waking nightmare.

Allie hadn't been back to the ship in what seemed like years. At first, after her arrival here, she had stayed near it, hoping for rescue but as the days turned into weeks, the ship had begun to morph before her eyes.

The smell of burnt flesh and cooked metal never fading away.

During her time near the ship, she had tried to bury as many bodies as possible but her strength gave out knowing there were parts of the ship she couldn't access. Those bodies had been left to rot, to become bones, until even those bones disintegrated into dust.

Being unable to find her friend's body amongst the dead still haunted her to this day. It was because of her that Allie ultimately stopped going back to the ship.

She had once crawled through the remains for supplies, for familiarity, and for the desperate hope of rescue. She had also stayed near it because she didn't know how to survive, and the monsters that came out at night frightened her.

But during her last visit to the ship, she had been looking for supplies that she may have missed from previous scavenging sessions and that she may have overlooked.

She had been deep within the confines of the wreckage when she heard a faint scratching noise behind her. When she had turned to look at what may have caused it, there was nothing there and the scratching had stopped.

At the time she had thought little of it– attributing it to critters or even the ship itself. But as she continued searching the rubble, the light, long scratches followed her. The longer she stayed in one area, the louder and closer it got.

Allie shivered from the memory.

She had stopped looking for materials at that point to listen to the scratches, trying to make sense of them. Testing them, they followed her from room to room.

The moment when her curiosity turned to terror with the realization that the noises were not from this world– that they were following her deliberately nearly broke her mind, as a breathless wail rose up behind her.

Her friend's face appeared before her, moving from the shadows as if it was drenched in sludge. She had been screaming and crying. Her long black hair losing itself in the ominous haze behind her, looming over her shoulders.

Allie ran.

She ran and hadn't stopped for days. She didn't stop until she stumbled past the crags and into the desert where she found her cave, staying there ever since.

Now she was going back and Allie couldn't decide if it was her need for companionship, her need to face her nightmares and make sense of them, or the thought of leaving Jack to face the ruins of the ship alone that had brought her on this path. Maybe it was all three.

Still, every step closer scared her. She glanced at Jack behind her and she knew she wouldn't let him go alone.

At that moment, he lifted his eyes and looked back at her. The day was half over now and if they kept walking, they would reach their destination sometime after nightfall.

Allie couldn't face that place in the dark, especially when it would be at its most powerful.

They looked at each other silently for a moment and she could tell he was assessing her. She had only been in his presence for a few days, but she was already used to the assessments. When his Cyborg-self came out and his human side receded into the background.

She still felt uneasy but now oddly reassured that he was there with her and that neither of them would have to face the darkness alone.

Still watching his eyes, it looked as if he was about to speak but stopped when she walked over to him and burrowed into his chest. She liked that he smelled of sweat and of heated metal, but also the very human scent of soap. She couldn't name the scent; she only knew that she liked it.

· · · ·

JACK HADN'T BEEN EXPECTING Allie's sudden change in mood. He instinctively put his arms around her, unsure of what else he could do. She was rigid in his arms.

As the day had gone on, he knew that something was up with her. Her demeanor had noticeably withered the closer they got to the wreckage. She must have been afraid of the memories that it was dredging up. That was natural after all – going through something traumatic and having to be reminded of it in such a harsh way would be difficult for even the bravest of men.

He tightened his hold on her, lifting her up slightly from the ground. "Allie, lift your legs up and hook them around my waist." He was going to carry her, since she needed comfort and he was willing to oblige. She wrapped her legs around him with little hesitation.

With her in his arms, he set about looking for a place for them to camp for the night. It was still early in the evening but they had walked all day without stop and had made good time.

It wasn't long before he found a small alcove that resembled a shallow cave. The entrance was partially obscured by a large rock, leaving them with protection from every side but the opening. There was enough space inside to accommodate their sleeping forms, a fire, and still have room to spare. He was pleased.

The girl hadn't lifted her head from the crook of his neck the entire time he scouted, trusting him to take care of her – or maybe she was so out of sorts that she didn't care.

Jack liked her there and he didn't want to disturb her; she was as much a comfort to him as he was to her at the moment. He gingerly shouldered off his pack to drop on the ground of their camp while holding her up with one arm. Once it was off, he sat with her against the wall, her legs straddling him. He synchronized his breathing to match hers.

They stayed like that for a short time. He took the much-needed break to run his fingers through her long hair, enjoying the feel of the silky strands, like water gliding over his skin.

She smelled like fear now, adding to her already enticing scent of woman, sweat, and sex. She perfumed the air around them and he couldn't get enough of it. He grabbed a handful of her hair and buried his face into it.

It was then that she looked up at him. "Jack. I'm afraid," she said, letting out a long breath.

"I know. You have been most of the day."

"Will you stay with me tomorrow?" she asked.

"I won't leave your side, but... I need to retrieve the parts. It means you'll have to enter the place. Unless you would like to stay here, I'll go ahead alone," he suggested, nuzzling her hair.

She shook her head, leaning back into him. "I know. I knew from the beginning I would have to go back there and enter. With you, I won't be alone, and neither will you."

"Gonna protect me from the ghosts?" he asked, trying to keep the amusement from his voice.

"You don't believe they exist. Hopefully, you're right and I'm just crazy." She sighed.

"I'll give you this, there is something strange with the wreckage. I have been monitoring it throughout the day and I have yet to get an accurate reading on it. I can't even tell the mechanical makeup of the vessel. You may not understand but that is very odd and rather unsettling for me. I can connect to machines, cybernetic engines, robotic networks, and I cannot connect to this one, whatever it is."

"You'll see for yourself tomorrow," she trailed off.

"I will."

They sat there for a short time lost in their separate thoughts. Jack knew now how hard tomorrow would be for her, and he would be with her through all of it. He wasn't going to lie to himself: the fact that he couldn't read the place troubled him. Every time he came close, it would slip away and the more he tried, the more frustrated he became.

The ship was, after all, a dead machine and even the dead could be read.

There was a point when a machine died, much like organic, biological life. When the wires, circuits, and connectors couldn't hold nor support a current. When the pieces rusted away, eroding with time or wear until nothing was left. And because he was a Cyborg, seeing that unnatural, mechanical death, a slow, sad burn death always left him feeling uneasy.

The state of perfection a distant memory.

He never wanted to experience that burnout. Losing your body was one thing. A Cyborg could upload his consciousness to the network, but to be denied that opportunity because your cybernetics died or they were no longer able to sustain you was like ceasing to exist. Once he and his brethren entered the world, they were meant to be there forever until otherwise killed or dismantled.

He watched as the sun began to set, the light striking the ground with an array of gold and bronze, reflecting off of the little crystals of sand. There was no green on this planet but the royal performance of the sun and sand more than made up for the lack of color. After his rather depressing thoughts, the sunset brought him back to the present, making the situation raw but hopeful.

Jack pulled his fingers away from the girl's hair and instead lifted her face to look at him. Her eyes were at half-mast and haunted. He ran the back of his index finger along her cheek. "Are you hungry?" he asked.

"No. I don't think I could eat even if I wanted to," she answered.

"Are you cold?" he asked her next.

"Not with your arms around me."

She was still covered up in her dingy rags, the cloak all but forgotten in his pack. He felt himself hardening.

"We'll set up camp for the night then," he said more as a statement and not a question. The least he could do was get her out of her head for a while, relieving his own pent up frustration to connect with her in the process.

She watched him as he reached over and pulled out her cloak and the two blankets from his pack, laying them out, overlapping them for extra padding from the stone ground. Once he was done, he lit a small fire on the opposite side of the alcove, conscious of keeping their exit open and unblocked.

While he was setting up their camp for the night, he watched Allie go over to the pack and rummage through his supplies. Amused, he watched her pick things up, look at them and then either place them back in the pack or on the ground. She looked excited by a small hair comb she found in one of the pockets, putting it aside for later no doubt.

Jack would have killed nearly anyone else who deemed it was within their rights to mess with his things. "What are you looking for?" He got up to crouch next to her.

"The cleaning cloth from earlier. I liked how it made me feel and I wanted to use it again before resting tonight," she said as she dug through the bag.

Jack laughed. Apparently she was looking forward to spending time with him tonight as much as he was. Her optimism was refreshing. "Here, let me get it." He reached in and retrieved the cloth and what he packed of the healing salve he had made her previously.

"Let me," he said, using this as a reason to touch her. He took her hand and ran the cloth along her skin, watching the sweat and dirt disappear. He would have to clean himself up too.

With deliberate slowness, he swiped the fabric up and down her sun-kissed arms. He took the time to caress it over each fingertip, moving up to the sensitive point between her fingers and ended with slow, soothing circles over her palms. She sat as still as stone and watched his every move.

When he let go of her hands, she took the chance to swipe her now soft tips over his brow, pushing his unruly hair to the side.

"Your eyes are always intense," she said.

"They often reflect my emotions, which are intense."

She smiled at him as she moved her hand away. He had wiped the cloth over her collarbone several times now, at a loss for which course of action he should take next.

Chapter Nine:

• • • •

Allie reached up and tugged the cloth out of his grip. He let it slip into her hand without resistance. She liked how he didn't seem so fierce when it was quiet and dark. When it was just the two of them in the gloom. She watched as he sat back on his heels and opened a disc of medicinal salve, similar to the one still in her pouch.

She unceremoniously wiped her face down, feeling instantly better. The magical cloth was a wonder of nature, looking down at it.

"The cloth is soaked in a mixture of nanoparticles that have attached themselves to salicylic acid. It helps remove the outer layer of your skin. The particles act as a catalyst and vaporize the dirt and toxins. It's something you can't see happening. The cloth only has so many uses before its effectiveness wears off. It's great as a temporary fix or for medical purposes, but overuse will dry out your skin."

"You don't mind that I'm using it?" Allie had been hoping for a more magical explanation.

"Not at all. That one will last for quite some time and I have a replicator back on my ship that can create more. They're great to have on hand when you're doing unconventional work." He smiled.

"Thank you," she said as she watched him unclip his armor, running his fingers over the buckles on his shoulder plates and biceps. They dropped off softly until all that was left was the under armor padding and mesh.

Jack was ripped with muscle but he wasn't large, instead tall and lean, like a man who could run for days, climb mountains, swim across large bodies of water. He looked nothing like the Warlord, whose body reminded her of the large boulders scattered about them.

Where the Usurper Warlord was meaty with muscle that was a battle cry to everyone within his presence, Jack was nuanced, dangerous, a harsh whisper, powerful and deadly. His body was built for performance and endurance. She had a hard time not staring at his chest.

He had been kind to her, provided for her, and even dealt with her emotional downpour earlier with patience. The few men she had encountered growing up at the colony were nothing like this man. Allie wanted him to touch her, to feel his hands glide all over her body, and she wanted to touch him back.

She moved toward him until she was a hairsbreadth away.

The way he was positioned, his back was mostly turned away from the fire and the light cast long shadows across his face. It distorted his features just enough so that she was unable to read his reaction clearly – if he had a reaction at all.

The sunlight had now dimmed to darkness and the temperature was dropping, but she barely noticed because, for once, their camp was warm and *she* was warm after nightfall.

With the fabric in one hand, Allie linked his fingers with her other and with care she began to clean him like he had done with her. Starting with his fingertips, over the palm, circling his large wrists and over his long, corded muscles.

Jack kept himself still and silent as she finished up with one arm and moved to the other, ending at his neck and hairline. When all of his exposed skin was clean, he reached down and pulled the under armor suit over his head, tousling his wayward dark locks in the process.

The deep shadows accentuated his body, caressing him much as she was planning to. Taking his action as approval, Allie began running the cloth over his chest. His skin was hot to the touch. His metalloid shell directly underneath. She paid special attention to his scars, outlining them with just a whisper of a touch.

He was settled on his knees now, his head bent forward just enough to let his loose strands fall before his eyes.

She couldn't tell if they were open or closed.

His chest was hairless. *His arms had been hairless too.* Allie looked over his body. It was a strong reminder that this man wasn't an ordinary man but a half man – a Cyborg – and comparing him to the men she had known before was wrong. There was no basis for comparison.

Allie took her time with every dip and groove, wanting this to be a pleasurable, relaxing experience for him. A way to thank him for going out of his way to comfort her.

Jack had had a tough life if his scars were any indication. She didn't bother to keep count of them, knowing that she wouldn't be able to do so. She had scars of her own.

I wonder if he has anyone? He was on that ship of his alone.

When she was done with his chest, she quietly moved to work on his back. Upon first inspection, it was similar to the front except for the tattooed numbers over his right shoulder blade. It had to be his identifying information. Allie couldn't understand what the numbers and symbols meant because it was in a foreign language, but she inherently knew that they had something to do with him being a Cyborg.

Once she finished with the initial wipe down, she dropped the cloth onto the pile of blankets at her side, taking up her exploration with her hands. He shifted as if he were about to get up.

"No. Don't move, yet. *Please*," she said quickly.

Jack turned to look at her briefly before settling back down. He busied his hands by unhooking his weapons that were strapped to his legs.

She took the opportunity to stroke her palms over his skin, adding pressure. It felt like human skin but without the minor imperfections and it felt strong, lacking the softness of body fat. His form was molded into the tightened confines of genetic perfection. It was velvety smooth to the touch, and very human goosebumps formed below her fingers as she continued.

Allie could feel the heady need of desire begin to grip her stomach, the yawning, aching emptiness grow between her legs. She pressed her thighs closed, knowing he could smell her based on their previous encounters; she was embarrassed. It was a lack of self-control, an insult to how she was raised.

They would touch but she wouldn't ask for more. Men chose their women, not the other way around – and she couldn't help the sad stray thought that she wasn't worth being chosen. A man, a Cyborg like Jack had a universe of options and she was only one woman of a countless many.

But she wouldn't ruin this moment with her thoughts.

Allie reached to the side where she had placed the small comb from earlier and sat up on her knees. With one hand placed on his shoulder for support she could feel him tense beneath her. Allie began running the comb through his dark, silky hair.

He groaned as she ran the bristles through, enjoying the tugging and untangling of small knots. She scraped his scalp just hard enough to send those electrifying sensations down his body. She felt those same sensations whenever he played with her long hair.

After several minutes of combing, he abruptly reached up and stayed her fingers.

"Stop," he said sternly.

She dislodged her hand and sat back on the blanket as he kneeled and stood up. Allie watched as he turned to face her, her will to breathe rapidly fading. He looked like a techno god, the shadows, and fire haloing his form.

"Take off your top." His eyes were charged with emotion. She hesitated, noticing the large erection tenting his pants. She was exhilarated and afraid. "I won't ask you again." His voice was laced with authority.

Allie took a deep breath and slipped the knot that kept her top in place and pulled it off her body. Her breasts exposed again for him in the firelight. Her nipples tightened under his gaze.

He reached down, grabbed the strip and tossed it in the fire.

She shot up, upset. "No!" Allie rushed to the flames but it was already too late. The cloth had disintegrated into ash.

"How could you? What am I supposed to wear now?" Allie turned to him, hurt, her mood ruined. *How dare he?!* She was being kind and he had ruined it.

"Not that piece of crap. I'll fashion you new clothes before we leave the camp tomorrow." He was being an asshole but he didn't seem to care. Allie bristled. Her clothes offered little protection but that wasn't by choice. They were all she had after so long on her own; everything else was destroyed by age and overuse.

She moved back to the blankets, skirting around his form, her arms crossed over her chest and picked up her cloak to cover herself, feeling sharp betrayal.

Allie flinched when he went over to her.

"You will have new, better coverings before we leave this cave, I promise. The rags you wear are old and provide little benefit to you." She didn't say anything but instead moved away from him.

• • • •

HE DIDN'T LIKE HER moving away. *She'll forgive me soon enough.* His body was alive with potent lust and he could still feel her fingers glide across his scarred chest. Jack had to stop *her* before he stopped himself. He didn't want to power down his humanity.

I just need to let go, see where this takes me.

He picked up the comb and his armor plates off the ground and placed them back into the pack, pulling out food and water in its place.

Jack handed over the nourishment in apology and held it in front of her for a few moments before she begrudgingly took it. He sat back and watched her eat, picking up one of his daggers. He twirled it against the stone floor, stabilizing his emotions. After a moment she looked at him.

"Are you going to eat?"

"No, I don't need food like you do," he answered.

She looked at him a moment longer and took a sip of water.

"Why do you do that? With the dagger that is, you play with it often." She watched as he ran his thumb along the sharp edge, tightening the cloak around her.

"Habit. It's safe to have a weapon in hand. I like the feel of it," he finished as he slid the edge over the pad of his thumb, drawing blood. "It reminds me that I'm human too."

They both stared as the blood welled up and dripped down.

"You've been hurt a lot?" She moved back to his side and held his hand between hers, oystering it, the pearl of his blood at the center.

"Quite a bit. The pain is a comfort now more than anything else."

"I think," she hesitated, "I understand. I've been alone for so long that feeling *anything* is better than feeling nothing at all. When you're alone for so long, it's the only thing to keep you company."

Jack wanted her more than anything at that moment. He didn't care anymore. They understood each other. He pulled her onto his lap, leaving a smear of blood along her skin. He lifted his thumb up to wipe it across her lips.

She dabbed at it with her tongue, scrunching her face.

He laughed at her reaction. "What? Don't like the taste of my blood? It's synthetic."

"No, not really." She swatted his hand away as he tried to smear more on her.

"But it makes your lips suicide red. My favorite color." He moved his hands up her thighs, reaching around to cup her butt and push her forward, into him.

Allie looked at him then with the blood around her lips. A little bit had trickled down over her chin. She looked like a vampiric vixen succubus; her hair a tangled mess around her face and down her back. Wild and primal and yet her eyes held a longing, desperate innocence.

And she was relaxed in his arms. Her trust in him was suffocating and very naive.

He moved his hands up her back until they were tangled in her sable hair. When she licked her lips, he grabbed it and pulled her forward, grinding his mouth against hers and after a moment she was kissing him as hard as he was kissing her. Their tongues at war. She bit down on his bottom lip, holding it in place as she ran her tongue along it. The taste of his blood in their mouths.

"You're getting better at kissing. I like the bloodplay." Jack moaned.

He kept one hand tangled in her hair while he roamed his other over her body, touching every part of her. His erection strained uncomfortably in his pants, feeling deprived of her pussy with the thin strips of cloth in his way.

She was on fire in his arms. Maybe Allie wasn't as innocent as he thought – her mind as messed up as his.

She was running her nails along his arms, leaving little red streaks in their wake. Her skin was inflamed, the heat between her legs like molten lava as the temperature in their little camp rapidly became unbearable.

• • • •

I NEED HIM. The pain of emptiness she harbored at her core tormenting her. *To hell with just touching.* She would take him regardless of her convictions. *He can be my warrior.*

Allie yelped when he tugged her head back, his hand in her hair tight and unrelenting, stopping herself from sneering at him. Using the opportunity to graze her nails down his hard chest with the need to add scars of her own.

"Sweetheart, lift your legs up." Jack was tugging at her covering. She moved onto her knees when he let go of her hair and tore the last remaining clothing she had, now completely stripped and in his lap and for once feeling no shame in her wantonness.

"God, you're so fucking beautiful." His eyes were shifting over her bare body, watching as he took her naked form into his memory or whatever Cyborg perusal voodoo Jack was doing. The golden light of the fire played over their forms.

He clasped her hips and brought her back down on his lap. Feeling his large manhood beneath her, she slid her fingers into his hair and ground herself against it, covering his pants in her dripping essence.

"Jack, I need you." She would beg him if she had to.

"I know, Allie, but if I don't slow down a little, I'll do things to you, to your cute little cunt, that you wouldn't like," he said as he looked down to watch her press into him. She followed his lead, watching herself practically mate him through his pants, not minding his veiled threat.

He reached down and pulled her lips apart, revealing her sensitive bud.

"You're hairless," he trailed off, rapt in examining her.

"I've been since my fertility testing."

"Damn. I'm going to butcher those men, bathe in their screams for touching you." His eyes shifted from intense to furious. "Fucking perverts."

"You don't like it?" She stopped moving against him long enough to focus on his statement.

"I love it. I just wasn't expecting it," he admitted.

She leaned forward and licked the scar on his lip. "It was a long time ago."

Jack kissed her roughly back as he pulled her flush against him, picking her up and laying her on the blankets. When she was spread out like a sacrifice, he kneeled up between her legs and unbuckled his pants, now moist from her core.

He dragged them down his hips, pulling his cock out with one hand while discarding them to the side. Her eyes went wide when she got her first view of it, cast in the dim light, staring at its size.

With a smirk he leaned over her, placing one hand next to her head to hold himself above her while his other stroked his deliciously large erection.

"Like what you see?" he asked, amused.

She felt like she was dying. He was so attractive, so masculine, her body cried for him to touch her as she watched him stroke himself above her. His once bloodied hand now constraining the head, massaging it with vigor as he stared down at her.

Allie moved her hand up over his shoulder and down his arm, around his fisted hand to grab the base of his cock, squeezing as he continued to play with himself. Jack groaned as she explored him, wondering if he was in as much pain to fill her as she was to be filled.

He let go of himself to place his hand beside her head, framing her face and holding himself above her form. The only place they touched was where her hand was rubbing his shaft.

What she thought might have been sweat dripped onto her face. "Ever been Cyborged, Allie?" His smirk widened into a full on grin.

"No?" she responded, confused and flushed.

"Didn't think so. You're about to be."

He sat back between her legs and glided his hands upward. He started with her feet, smoothing over her calves, whispering his fingers behind her knees before snaking his hands up between her thighs. Her legs fell open, exposing everything to his gaze.

He leaned down and breathed her in and he continued to do it several times, his face entranced from her scent.

Jack's fingers caressed upward until she nearly bolted off the floor when he pushed her feminine lips wide open. She felt his hot breath skate across the sensitive skin.

"These lips were made for kissing."

She should have been appalled but she wasn't, instead wanting to beg him to do it, feeling so lost in the sensation that she wanted to melt into his touch.

Is he really going to kiss me down there? She squirmed when his thumb slid along her taut skin.

He spread her wetness from her core up to her clit, where he rubbed it slowly, ending with a tight pinch. Her hips jumped off the blanket, her knees bent up, her hand rose up to tangle in his hair. Jack didn't kiss her or lick her but brutally pinched her, and with each pinch her body spasmed. Her focus zeroed in on the tension building between her legs when he abruptly penetrated her core with a finger from his other hand.

"Your pussy is soaking, sweetheart. It's so tight, I may rip you open." He moaned but said in all seriousness, "We wouldn't want that now."

He let go of her clit and wrapped his arm under her writhing body, lifting her up and impaling her on his finger.

He slammed it deep inside her until his hand was coated with her pussy, and when he thrust up a second finger, anchoring her body onto them, she lost it, falling against him as a ripple coursed through her system. She was so sensitive that her body wanted to jerk away and regroup but he kept her in place, his fingers scissoring and probing her core.

His tempo only increased as he continued to penetrate her, her sensitivity levels uncomfortable. She heard her herself beg him to stop but he didn't listen. Instead, he opened her up, coaxed her essence and spread it all over. Now and again feeling his rough thumb circle her opening.

Jack lifted her up and placed her core right above his straining cock. She barely registered that she was going to be impaled on it and not his fingers in the next moment.

She felt his tip enter her, stretching her out, demanding entrance into her body and in one quick thrust upward, he broke her open. "Jack!" Allie squeaked out in shock.

• • • •

JACK LOST CONTROL. Allie was bucking, clawing at him, trying to pry herself away but he wouldn't let her. She was his now, whether she liked it or not. Her struggles only made him want to subdue her more.

He held her on his shaft until she sagged against him in defeat. He tried hard not to pound into her, to lose himself in her tight sheath.

"Why?" she cried.

He lifted her chin to face him while he continued to hold her on him. "Because it was inevitable. It always hurts the first time."

"This isn't my first time," she sniffled, her eyes welling up. Her tears hurt him but enticed him with their delicious salty smell.

"You told me you had never been raped." His ardor turning to boiling hot rage.

"I wasn't. I took my own virginity years ago." She shook against him, relaxing slowly, he didn't miss the blush that crept over her cheeks.

"Taking it yourself is not the same as being with a man or a Cyborg. This is still your first time, regardless of any barriers being breached." He pushed up into her slightly.

She was no longer trying to get away, so he released her to wipe the tears off of her face.

"If you give it some time," he gritted his teeth, "it will feel good." He pushed up into her again. Allie was so tight, he thought his cock might lose circulation. He should have been slower, he knew, but he needed to be inside her. Bottoming out may not have been the best idea for her first time; still, he couldn't bring himself to regret it.

"It hurts. It hurt before... not being filled. But this hurts just as much," she whispered, her hands clinging to him.

She wasn't moving so he would have to do it for her. The only way she would start to feel good again was if he could stimulate her. He captured her hips and began to move them slowly up and down, now and again changing the motion to circle them. Allie felt so hot on him, he wanted to fall back, and groaning, he imagined her riding him without restraint.

After a moment of the light movements, she initiated the sway herself, getting a feel for it, and soon after he was blessed with a breathy moan.

"That's it, sweetheart, move on me."

She grabbed his shoulders and leaned in, biting his scarred lip so hard she drew blood.

I deserved that.

He lifted her up and she pushed back down as they increased their tempo in unison.

"This does feel good," she moaned.

It wasn't long before they were slamming into each other. The only noises in the small alcove were their heavy breaths and the slap of their skin. He helped her ride his cock, keeping his grip on her hips strong, keeping her going whenever she began to tire. His erection felt strangled.

Jack watched as her head fell back, her hair tickled his legs as she pushed her breasts out and as he moved her on him. His gaze fixated on her bouncing tits, each bounce in sync with their bodies joining.

Her nipples were soft, pink, and tight, like little raspberries. He would never look at a raspberry again without thinking of her tits.

Her stretched out cunt was quivering. "Come. Now," he demanded, knowing she was on the brink. She exploded in his arms, losing control, pressing her legs together firmly against his thighs to hold him in place as she thrashed out above him and when her climax subsided, he pushed her back onto the blankets and fucked her small body, forcing her to take his brutality, cumming in her relentlessly until he slowly softened his thrusts and his cock twitched with the last of his release.

When he was done, and by the time he lifted away, she was nearly passed out in sleep. She smiled up at him, moaning and reaching for him to return.

He stroked her body as he reached for the discarded cleaning fabric and wiped himself down before he gently pried her legs open. He cleaned her up, watching as his cum beaded and leaked out of her before vaporizing.

Mine. He circled her swollen core with his finger. *Mine.* A repeated mantra in his head.

"Mmm, Jack. Thank you," she said sleepily.

He didn't respond, letting her drift off. He slathered the medicinal salve he had over his fingers and spread it over her glistening, reddened lips, her entrance, before fingering her for the second time that night to apply the solution inside her. He hardened again.

Softly, as not to disturb her, he spread her legs wider to his gaze and kneeled between them. With his hand clenched around his swelling dick, he ran its head up and down her core until he was once again coated in her dew.

With a frustrated groan, his tip straining against her opening, he lifted away. Jack jerked himself off as he imagined penetrating her for the second time that night. Fantasizing that she would wake up with his cock pushing into her.

Her wide bottomless eyes would open in shock.

A heavy gasp that would quickly become a moan would escape her lips.

Her long, lithe legs would hook around his back.

He moaned when his cum shot out. He grabbed the cloth and cleaned himself up for the second time as he pushed Allie's legs back together. When he was done, he laid himself beside her and tucked his body behind her back, moving her into a spoon position, cocooning her frame.

A short while later he drifted off to sleep.

Chapter Ten:

• • • •

Allie was so warm, so constricted. She took inventory of her body as the fogginess of sleep receded. Her muscles ached and stretched in many places but she didn't bother to open her eyes, knowing it was still dark, that she hadn't been asleep for long.

The fire had died down to a single flame.

But it was still bright enough to flicker behind her eyelids at random intervals.

She knew where she was and who was wrapped around her, his breathing even and predictable. His hard chest pushed into her back with each breath and his breath was whispering over her ear, the warm air tingling her skin.

His arm was around her in a vice-like hold and it was the only thing that was covering her naked form. His body was hot like an overheated machine and it was better than any blanket she had ever had. Their position was comfortable.

Allie was tired and still half asleep as she counted his breaths, listening to every slight rustle of their bodies – aware of his semi-hard erection between her buttocks. She wanted him again even though she was still sore, the salve still working between her legs, the cooling sensation a relief.

She was wicked – the pain they had shared together had driven her beyond any normal reason. Drawing his blood, attacking his skin with her nails, a canvas for her pent up emotions spoke to something she kept hidden deep inside.

Just as she began to drift back into a dreamy state of being, the light flickered as if it was hit by an invisible breeze, catching her attention. Allie peeked her eyes open to focus on it, tuning out her previous thoughts, her awareness of the dim glow and Jack's breathing fell away.

The silence became hollow around her as if there was no place for the rest of the world. The absence pushed it away.

She couldn't comprehend the sudden change that fell over the camp; it was as if the gloom had perforated the space naturally, a strange dark mist. She could feel a tension build around her, sucking the air out and making it hard to breathe.

Her stomach dropped and Jack's arm around her no longer felt safe but began to feel like a restraint. Her heart beat elevated, feeling fast and erratic. Not being able to move, she watched as the flame flickered and faded before her eyes. It pitched the cave into an unnatural darkness.

She was no longer warm and comfortable, but terrified and faint.

The sound of quiet breathing morphed into long, unnatural scratching. The direction of the scratching was out of her vision, the grotesque, sharp noise came from the unguarded entrance at her head.

Allie shut her eyes.

No. No. No.

She didn't want to see it, hearing the long, perverted screech move closer. If she saw it, she knew her mind would snap. That her life would be altered forever and in a terrible way. She wouldn't come back from this.

The scratching moved closer, bringing the weight of darkness with it, drowning out everything else.

A gurgling, pitched hum was right before her now, and the grinding claws came to a halt. The smell of rot filled her nostrils. Something was between her and the dead flame. She wanted to scream, run, tear something apart but she was paralyzed. She closed her hand into a fist, digging her nails into her palm when the humming abruptly stopped.

"Allie, don't open your eyes."

She nearly jumped out of her skin at Jack's whisper. Was he crazy too? His arm held her tight into him, shielding her. He moved above her, putting himself between her and where the creature had been.

When he let go, she curled up into herself, bringing her head to her knees. The stifling atmosphere depressurized around her.

Allie heard him get up and she opened her eyes to scream at him to run, to watch out, but the cave filled with a glorious burst of light before she could. Jack had lit the fire, banishing the dark thing that had crawled its way in.

She burst into tears.

He moved over to her and lifted her into his lap, and she felt the weight of his dagger pressed into her skin. He had armed himself; perhaps the creature hadn't been a figment of her imagination but was real. She felt reassured by that notion, but the tears kept flowing and she couldn't stop herself from sobbing.

She felt his hands on her back, drifting up and down her spine and after some time her tears ran out, an age-old tiredness overtook her. The weight of all her spiraling emotions seeped out of her like her tears, leaving nothing left but a numb, empty shell.

I'm not going crazy. There was something that came into the camp and Jack had seen it. She hadn't looked but she had felt it, heard it. The realization was powerful, knowing her internal struggles had become physical ones.

That there was something physical haunting her and Jack had *seen* it and that meant maybe it could be killed. That she could be free of it. A sliver of hope blossomed in her heart.

Allie remembered the thing now. It had approached her once before, long ago, and it wasn't her friend. It wasn't her guilt and shame taking form, it was something else... Why else would the creature appear now? So close to the wreck?

Darkness had visited her often in her cave but it was just that, just darkness. The ghoul had never appeared with it before. Was it bound to the ship? The dead? She was suddenly very happy that she had run so far away years ago, comforted that it couldn't reach her easily.

Jack had seen it, had put himself between her and the creature. How could she ever repay him? He was her hero. She wanted to feel close to him again, burrowing her face into his neck and sucking on his skin, licking it, getting his taste back in her mouth. His arms slid off her as he wrapped his hands around her upper arms, silently urging her on.

He was hard and probing beneath her, and she noticed him lengthen and thicken even more. Allie moved her lips over his neck and along his chin until she caught his mouth to slide her tongue along his, emboldened by his groan. His hands tangled in her hair, tugging it.

She reached down and rubbed his shaft, simultaneously positioning herself over it. She heard her name whispered on his lips.

Allie slid down on it, fitfully, until she was flushed against him, filled with him. *I can't get close enough.*

They stayed like that, kissing in desperation, her body bouncing on him intermittently until the sun crested the horizon. Both of them abstaining from their climax until the cave was filled with the light of dawn, until every shadow had vanished.

And when it was filled, he laid her down on the ground and pounded into her, both of them erupting into flames until there was nothing left but mindless desire and need.

Chapter Eleven:

• • • •

Jack was at a loss. He should have been sated, having Allie in his arms all night, and under any other circumstances he would have been, but the itchy sensation that it was clouded by something abnormal bothered him.

They had been visited by something supernatural, something evil, and it frayed his senses. The thing hadn't left after he relit the flame, but stayed in the shadows beyond them and watched. He couldn't read it but he felt its presence until the night's end.

He had been sleeping one moment and the next... his sensors woke him up, they notified him to the girl's dangerously elevated heart rate. Her fear.

He had no notion of there being something else with them, he had felt and sensed nothing and that had never happened before. Cyborgs were configured like an alarm system, anything, everything triggered them, alerted them.

It wasn't until he opened his eyes that he saw it, just feet away from them – a stringy creature with dead eyes had been leering at Allie.

The thing had long sinewy arms as if they had been stretched to the point of falling off. They hung limply by its sides. Long, sharp, grey-tipped claws dragged along the floor behind it, and it had been crouching close to the ground as if it crawled to its location.

But it was the face that felt like a kick to the gut. Dead, hungry eyes, looking at her, not even aware of his presence. A twisted, sick grin with sharp and broken incisors filled its mouth.

The thing just stayed where it was, staring in hungry glee, feeding off of her terror.

And when he leaned in and whispered in her ear, it slithered into the shadows, deforming before his eyes.

He wasn't prepared for this. And that made him angry. After the thing had slithered back to where it had crawled out from, he had wanted to chase it down and stab the creepy grin off of its face. The only reason he hadn't made such a move was because the girl was about to shatter.

If Jack based his assumption on her reaction to the monster – the fact that she was desperately trying to deny its presence, her eyes closed tight, her face creased in fear – this wasn't the first time she had encountered the creature. It had been focused on her, it wanted her, it had stared at her like it had finally won.

Like hell it had.

He was going to hunt the creepy piece of shit down and carve a trophy out of its saggy skin, if not for frightening the girl, then for sneaking up on him.

After he had relit the fire, he reconnected his transmission lines to the intergalactic network, searching the grid for its description in angry silence. Uploading his images of the creature to run a diagnostics for similar matches. There was always something out there to learn. Nothing new existed that wasn't a part of the network, at least not for long.

His results were worthless speculations, crazed reports, random folklore and all of it originating from Earth, the homeland. No facts, no science.

What he had accumulated was mythos from archaic religions, and so he decided that the thing must be native to this planet and was from no such fairytale. It was the most logical assumption. *Demons, my ass.*

The most unnerving part thought was that it didn't exist on his radar. Jack couldn't scan it, read it, analyze its strengths and weaknesses, and even now, searching for it, nothing blipped on his trackers. It had appeared in their cave as if out of nothing and it remained that way.

A *Nothing* didn't inhabit this infested planet.

All he had to go on was his gut reaction and he didn't want to admit it, his sixth sense. If he hadn't laid his eyes on it, he would have never believed that it existed.

He looked over at Allie, now dressed in his under armor, sipping from a water canister. His thoughts changed direction. It was only an hour after the sun had risen, and her skin was still painted with a rosy flush while the smell of their sex still perfumed the air.

She had approached him last night like it was her only link left with sanity. He could sense the quiet desperation in her to connect with him. He wasn't surprised that she needed the contact so badly, and his chest tightened uncomfortably with the thought.

He had never been needed, not at an emotional, physical, individual level, and her need had been heady for him, he wanted to harness it: keep it in a bottle and lock it away someplace where he could covet and protect it.

It could become an addiction.

When he had taken her to the ground earlier, he had been coming off a high. He had been useless for anything else at that moment, and losing himself was all he could do. Even now he wanted to take her again, to reclaim that need and her body.

But he couldn't, at least not right now. He strapped his guns on, one across his back and the pistol belted on his waist. He watched her get up and come over to him, the water canister in her hand now depleted. He pulled out one of his spare daggers and handed it to her.

"Take this. Stab anything that moves that isn't me," he warned her as she took it from him.

"I will, but I don't think it will help." Jack knew what she meant.

"I have a .44 pistol. You can carry that instead if you like."

She looked at him strangely, "I don't think that will help either. I don't know how to use a gun. I would most likely shoot you."

"Oh, sweetheart, you're breaking my Cyborg heart. When we pick up the metal and my ship is repaired, I'm going to teach you how to shoot every gun in my armory." He sighed.

"If you trust me enough not to kill you, I would like that, although a gun wouldn't be useful here. There's nothing to shoot at but rocks and dirt."

"There's always something that needs a bullet in it, and trust me, you've got bloodlust in that body of yours, you're going to love it. I'll even let you keep your favorite one," Jack offered.

Allie gave him a pointed look, "I don't think I agree with you about the blood."

His grin widened. "If you weren't so damn sore and if we didn't want to get this little adventure behind us so badly, I would take you up on your lusty offer." He laughed, feeling his cock twitch in anticipation.

"Who says I'm sore?" she asked sweetly.

His grin faded and he squinted his eyes at her in suspicion. "I know you're sore and I know you're stalling. Let's just get this over with so I can lock you up in my cabin, preferably by tomorrow night. Now let's go."

He watched her face drop.

"Nothing will happen to you. I won't let it. Like I said, stab anything that moves that isn't me and don't leave my side. I mean it, Allie, aim to kill." He picked up the pack and hefted it onto his back. Unconsciously, he reached over and took her hand.

• • • •

ALLIE MATCHED HIS STRIDE and walked beside him. They would be at their destination by mid-morning and she felt strangely calm about it; Jack seemed assured and that made her feel better.

He would retrieve what he needed and then they would leave. She would be heading back through here this afternoon, knowing she would never see the ominous ship again. The thought was liberating and a wave of giddiness shot through her.

By tonight she would be on her way home, she would be with Jack again, and in several days she would have her supplies – her soap – and be able to go back to her daily routine. She would take him up on his offer to learn how to shoot if it still stood.

He would repair his ship. He would leave.

She would be alone again. Allie looked over at him. Would she be able to cope, being alone again? Imagining her days without him shot a dart through her heart. She would try to manage the loneliness and when enough time had gone by, she would accept his absence. Everything would be like it had been. Like it had been a week ago.

Allie would be a moment in his life and he would be a moment in hers. She just wasn't sure if a moment was long enough for her. Their hands were still clasped and she squeezed his in reassurance of her feelings. She felt his fingers, threaded through hers, squeeze her back.

I don't want to be alone anymore.

The thought of her old life was painful. The endless, unchanging days, the constant worry of starving, getting hurt, being buried alive. The nights and the darkness that followed. Maybe instead of supplies, she could ask for passage to some other place, some safe place.

That alternative frightened her too, because she wasn't sure how to reintegrate into a society. Even the draped armor mesh falling around her form felt foreign. And she was fertile, so if she returned to society she would be expected to join with an Earthian or Trentian male and reproduce. Both species were still struggling to rebuild after the war.

She focused on their linked hands. It reminded her of Ophelia. Allie pushed the memory away.

She wanted Jack but she would not place the burden of her wants on his shoulders.

Allie knew very little about Cyborgs, only that they were created during the war, for the war. That they were not a species of their own, and only a finite number of them were in existence. Would it be possible for a relationship to form between them when he was on a different level of existence than she was?

Jack was now holding her hand, a deeply human thing to do.

"We're getting close." He interrupted her thoughts, squeezing her hand before letting go as if he knew she had been focused on it. "We'll make this quick. I'm going to harvest some metal plating and any palladium circuitry. I'll have to get to the atomic reactor if it's still there, turn it on, and see if there is any power left. The power will help me identify where the circuits are. If that doesn't work, we'll move on to plan B."

"Plan B?" She was curious, missing the connection.

"Dig for the circuits. It would take longer."

"There's no other way?" Allie didn't want it to take longer.

"I could send out a distress signal but we could attract unwanted visitors, or no visitors at all. This place is so far outside of the normal space sectors, those that would see my signal are more likely to be my enemies than not. I could send a transmission to my brethren but it may take weeks or months for one to get here. I don't have time to wait."

Allie wanted to ask him to elaborate on why he was in a hurry, but they crested a hill and found themselves on a plateau, overlooking the ship. The conversation dropped.

The ship hadn't changed.

It was exactly how she remembered it the last time she had been here. The only differences were that it appeared to be sinking into the hole it created upon impact, and it was covered in thick layers of sand and dirt. Time itself was trying to bury the monster.

It looked like a shipwreck but it felt like a nightmare. The monochrome metal was now shades of pasty grey, like a corpse. There were large plates of metal peeling away like sunburnt skin, and those plates protruded it as if they had a mind of their own, one that wanted to be away from the main vessel as much as she did.

The entirety of it stuck out of the ground at a sloping angle. It was a bruise amongst the golden landscape. The ship didn't belong and it never could, even with the camouflage of sand that adhered to it.

The ground around it was littered with debris from the impact, large metal plates that had fallen off to entire sections of the ship that had detached. She remembered many of the forms from long ago. Unlike the main perversion, the debris looked like unwanted cast-offs, not part of the land but also not part of the ship. They were orphans to two dangerous entities.

And the smell...

Allie couldn't understand how it was possible that it still reeked of the same burned flesh, rotting bodies, and the tang of rust from when it first crashed here. Even from a distance, the smell was strong as if the structure had been suspended in time.

She wanted to vomit up the water sloshing in her belly, thankful now that she had not bothered to eat any rations earlier.

Jack was a statue next to her, the sun glinting off his guns. He stared daggers at the ship, not moving to hurry her up to get this ordeal behind them like he had urged all morning. Allie knew he was stuck in his head, analyzing what was before them and solidifying his opinion.

She wrapped her fingers around the hilt of the dagger that was now tied to her waistband and pulled it free.

A weapon is better in hand.

The metal cooled her clammy palm and was a small comfort as her connection to Jack faded and her connection to the ship before her strengthened. The dagger was a physical reminder that she wouldn't be alone.

Leaving Jack where he was standing, she carefully descended into the valley below, scaling the rocky ledges and loose sand. She didn't need to form an opinion; she already had one.

As she made her way toward her past, the ship became unsettlingly bigger, blocking out everything around it as it filled her vision. The air was heavy with memories, and the oppression of them was building, weighing down on her shoulders as she got closer. Each step felt like coals beneath her feet.

Allie noticed that the sand and dirt changed color as she got closer. What had been golden brown was now muddied streaks of dark grey mixed with black, webbing outward like an infection in the bloodstream. It continued until everything she stood on was black.

Could this place get anymore diseased?

She was at the bottom now, looking up at the ship instead of looking down. She moved around it, sizing it up, at the same time making her way to her destination.

Off to the side from where she and Jack had come from was a colossal rock. Her feet sank into the sand as she approached it. The rock was a giant gravestone to all the mangled corpses she had buried there. The ground below her a gravesite.

She knew the bodies were long gone, that only bones remained, but the ever-present smell of death was incredibly strong here. She could barely breathe, and looking down, all she saw was the darkened sand.

She was struck with a wave of guilt, and sadness. How come everyone had died but she had lived? How was that possible? *I had walked away from the destruction with barely a scratch when everyone around me was broken and burned.*

Her friends had perished, the innocent crew had perished, the noble captain who saved their lives had perished. Better people had died and she had lived, and it hurt her heart.

Being alone on this planet was her punishment for defying death.

Allie kneeled down in the dirt and grabbed fistfuls of it into her hands, desperately seeking forgiveness – knowing it would never come. It didn't want forgiveness; it wanted revenge. She could feel its anger beaming into her, weighing her down.

Jack's familiar presence approach behind her. His hand covering her shoulder. She picked up the dagger she had dropped in the dirt and stood up, brushing the sand off of her legs before turning around to face him.

"This is where I buried the bodies," she confessed numbly. "At least, the ones I could find…"

He folded her into his arms. "It's not safe here," he said as he led her away from the grave pit. Allie didn't turn to look at it again.

• • • •

JACK UNDERSTOOD WHY he was unable to get a feel for the place before. The ship was pulsating dangerously strong magnetic ripples and it screwed up the readings on several of his systems.

He had yet to find an explanation for the strange waves, but it was obvious to him that a strong, mystifying force surrounded the ship. And if he wasn't careful, his cybernetics could be irreversibly affected. Luckily, so far nothing within him was screaming a warning.

The dirt that Allie grabbed, that now clung to her fingers and palms, had been dyed from the old metal plating. The color appeared to be melting off and into the immediate environment.

There was no other logical explanation and he refused to believe that anything was inexplicable. There will always be an explanation, as long as you had the right knowledge, the right resources.

Jack was grasping at straws. *Why would the metal change the color of the sand?*

When the ship had come into view, he hadn't expected to find a battlecruiser, not unlike the ones flown during the war, but had expected to find a transporter vessel, one that may have been modified with foreign enhancements. He was familiar with this ship, the mechanics, the design, the parts. He would find what he needed here to repair his own.

The cruiser was slowly sinking into the ground.

Even now he could feel the shift of sand beneath his feet as it was being pulled under by the caverns of old wurm tunnels below, resulting in a large but rather slow pit of quickening sand.

He held onto Allie as he approached the exterior where a large triangular hole had broken open. The tough metal split outward as if something had violently forced its way out.

Stopping in front of the gaping hole, he peered inside and saw a corridor of debris that stretched out into a tunnel on the opposite end, leading deeper into the ship. Long metal tubing hung limply from the walls and ceiling. The tubes were no longer vital to the ship's life like they had been at one point, operating on electrical currents, controlled by the ship's engines.

Jack pressed his free hand on the dingy plating, trying to make a connection with the vessel, but found only silence. His nanobots were rejected by the lifeless structure in his effort to bring it to life. It had been inert for over half a decade.

The girl had been alone longer than he originally had thought based on the ship. He looked down at her, "How old were you when you crashed here?" he asked, curious about her past.

She looked at him in confusion. "Based on the colony's planet rotation, I was seventeen cycles."

The cycles on this planet were longer than an average Earth day, he estimated that she was in her mid-twenties. "This ship crashed here about seven cycles ago, standard Earthian time six and a half years. You've been here a long time." Jack was proud of her survival instinct before but now he was impressed. She had been here for a quarter of her lifespan. One mystery solved.

Allie let go of him to run her hands through her hair, her eyes wide and sad with the knowledge. He fell silent as she processed the information.

"There are no seasons here. I knew I had been here a long time but I was never able to accurately track it. I tried at first but I stopped when it didn't seem to matter anymore. No one was coming. Eventually the days began to blur together."

"I came."

She looked at him sadly. "Not by choice."

"Maybe not by choice, but instead by fate. If I knew you were stranded here, I would have come by choice. I would have been here years ago. If I knew you existed, I would have slaughtered your Warlord before he ever laid eyes on you and gifted you with his head."

Allie stood before him awkwardly and obviously unsure about how to respond to his confession. "He was never my Warlord," she eventually stated.

Jack frowned and turned back to the ship, "I'm going to harvest the palladium first. It will be abundant near the core. On our way out, I'll extract the metal since that can be taken from anywhere." He stepped into the dank corridor, hearing the girl quietly follow him in.

The atmosphere abruptly changed and he would have likened it to the strange magnetic fields surrounding the area but that would have been impossible. He felt like he was in a pressurized bubble. A chill clung to the air where just steps back he had been enveloped in warm, direct sunlight.

The temperature shouldn't have plummeted so dramatically. Jack scanned the atmosphere. *No irregularities.* He knew the girl would be uncomfortable as it was uncomfortable even for him.

Jack pulled out her cloak and draped it around her shoulders, securing it in place.

"It smells terrible in here. It was foul outside but this..." she trailed off. He couldn't smell anything. Just the sweat on their bodies and the waning scent of sex from earlier; her essence dried over the crotch of his pants.

Allie had her hand over her nose, her eyes pinched tightly closed. He could sense her growing wariness.

He rummaged through his pack and pulled out a flashlight and handed it to her. "You'll need this. We won't have much light going forward." She let go of her nose, wrinkling it, and took the light from him.

"Thank you." Allie held it to her chest as he replaced the pack on his back.

Jack moved deeper in, keeping a hand running along the wall of the passage and keeping his connection with the vessel. He mapped out the ship's interior layout and plotted the quickest path to the reactor. There were several barriers in the way, but nothing that he couldn't manage.

They would be climbing steadily upward as the nose of the battle cruiser had been all but destroyed in the dirt from the impact. What remained of the cockpit was now buried in layers of dead ground.

Lucky for me, what I need is in the middle-rear of the ship.

The light from the entrance had diminished and continued to fade as they made their way steadily deeper. He heard Allie click the flashlight on behind him and a second later a bright ray of white light pierced through the dusty gloom. It made the space around them a monochrome, stale grey that had contrasted deep black shadows. Dull reflections bounced off the dirty chrome of the wires and walls.

He looked behind, the natural light was but a dot of color at the end of the tunnel, obstructed by the pipes hanging off of the ceiling. Allie followed his gaze and noticeably shivered.

This place looked like somewhere the creature from earlier would inhabit; it was as creepy and messed up as its wide, broken grin.

Jack switched his vision partially to night while he left his other eye on infrared. There was nothing alive in this place, but he knew it never hurt to be careful.

He moved forward.

They steadily made their way through, stopping now and again for him to dislodge or destroy obstructions in their way, breaking through rusted-out panel doors and helping Allie over dangerous sections. The ship was larger than his own by quite a bit; it was meant to maintain weaponry as well as a large crew, whereas his could be comfortably operated by a crew of one.

The flyer wasn't big by normal battle cruiser standards. This one would have been an outlier to the usual World Eaters the military used. People lived and died on World Eaters. Regardless, he was pleased with the progress they were making.

A startled gasp sounded behind him, and the direction of the light no longer pointed forward. The beam had landed on a mass of human remains. He walked closer but didn't need to use his scanners on them, as the grouping was large enough to be from several bodies.

"They're in a pile. I never left bodies I found in this ship, let alone in a pile," she whispered, a hitch in her voice. He moved closer to them and kneeled down. His arm rested on his knee while he unsheathed his dagger to move the bones apart.

"They were placed here deliberately. It looks like they were discarded."

"I would never. Not with the dead," she breathed.

"I know, sweetheart. If I thought you could do something like this, I would never have slept next to you." Jack laughed lightly, hiding his growing concern.

"Don't laugh about this. If it was deliberate, who did it?" He could tell her question was rhetorical but he answered anyway.

"It doesn't matter, these bones were moved here long ago. Whatever did this is long gone. We're alone on this ship." He got up and moved away, disturbed. "Let's keep moving. I want to be out of here by this afternoon and we're almost to the core."

He placed his hand on her arm and led her quickly away. Jack did not want Allie to see what he had.

That there were long perforations in the bones as if something ate the meat off of them and then continued to chew them down, that some pieces had entire chips bitten off while other had long claw marks along their sides as if sharp teeth had been scraped across them.

He concluded that it could have been done by the creature from last night. He was unable to get it out of his head, perusing the images over and over. The broken and sharp teeth came to mind, the similarities convenient. He filed away the new information to investigate later.

The reactor and the circuitry were just beyond the wall before him now. He dropped his hand away from the girl and felt around the cool metal for any weaknesses, locating several soon after. Jack shrugged out of his pack again and sheathed his dagger.

"Stand back," he ordered, hearing her move away.

He placed his hands over the frail metal and forcefully transferred his nanorobotics into it like he had earlier, but this time programming them for deterioration. It wasn't long before he was able to transfer enough into the wall before him; he watched the metal visibly rust away.

Jack moved his hands and let the bots do their job. The place his hands had just touched crumbled into a small gap. The fragments fell away. When it was wide enough for him to thread his fingers through, he gripped the edges and broke apart the decaying wall, helping its demise along.

Taking the opportunity to store some of the larger broken pieces away, he strapped them to the outside of his pack.

Allie had moved forward to shine a light on the disappearing wall, and he sensed her heartbeat increase.

"It's like magic. How did you do that?" She stepped back as he tore off a large chunk and set it aside.

"I transferred some of my biomechanical cells into it. They're programmable and always a part of me wirelessly until they dissipate. They can fix, destroy, scan, or take over other things," he said. "They can't take over inanimate objects like this wall but they can take it apart."

"Can you transfer them to people and change them?" she asked cautiously. He knew why, referring to inserting them into her days prior.

"Yes and no. They can't change organic material that has a different genetic makeup than mine. Eventually, they would be attacked and destroyed. My nanocells don't last long outside of my body."

"What about the yes, though?"

He looked over at her. "If I wanted to impregnate a woman, then they would align with the female's egg, altering the genetic code but also altering their own over the maturation period. Any child procreated by a Cyborg is born with their own naturally designed nanocells. It was a byproduct of our production. Unknown until after we were created."

"There are Cyborg children?" Her mouth had dropped open.

"Yes but they're not Cyborgs, the children are human but genetically enhanced. They also always look similar to the original host of the nanocells. They're a secret, so few exist that the council is not aware of their existence. It's a secret we all keep."

"Why?" she asked.

"That type of technology requires a lot of money and a lot of time and resources. To create nanocells that are compatible with a human is difficult and expensive. I'm a difficult, expensive machine to create. Could you imagine what would happen if they had inexpensive access to that technology? I prefer not to find out." Jack turned back towards the collapsing wall. "We Cyborgs have a tense relationship with our creators. We're free because we're men and women who our freedom with blood and pain. Some would prefer us decommissioned or enslaved. We try to kill those people off when we can," he stated ominously. The hole was now big enough to walk through. They moved into the armored core.

Jack bent to work on powering up the reactor, slowly feeling the beginning vibrations of electrical currents pulsating outward. The ship was coming to a half-life state of being. Several minutes passed before Allie spoke again.

"Does the council still make Cyborgs?"

"They do but very few. We call them Neoborgs and they're not really trustworthy. The Neoborgs are not created for war like the originals were, like me. They usually have unique purposes. Mainly it's just a creation to enhance humanoid knowledge or new processes being tested, new information. Neoborgs are built mainly for intellectual enhancement and theory."

Her fingers landed on his forearm as he turned away. "Jack..." the girl whispered. He looked back at her, concern and wonder painted her face. He felt enchanted and leaned to kiss her when she spoke, stopping him in his tracks.

"Could I be pregnant?" His internal systems felt like they were crashing around him and he was suddenly aware of how inappropriate this conversation was deep inside a dead machine that was littered with bones.

He looked at her stomach before lifting his gaze back to her face. A look of concern clouded her eyes as she waited for his answer; he watched as she began to notice the stifling metallic rust around them.

"You're not pregnant."

A small smile lifted her lips and he felt compelled to kiss her again. "Oh. Good. I don't think I'm ready yet."

Without turning back toward her, he lowered his voice in authority, "Keep an eye out. I'm going to need to focus on retracting the circuits. Any other time this would not be an issue but the ship is scrambling my electrical signal and I can only surmise that it will be more powerful now that I'm next to the reactor and it's powering on. If you see or hear anything, yell." Jack ducked under a metallic band-like barrier, losing his view of the girl. "This shouldn't take me long. When the ship starts to power off, you'll know that I'm done." He kneeled down and looked at her from under the barrier. "Kiss me."

He watched as she stepped closer to him, gingerly bending down with that small smile on her face. Right before their lips met, he grabbed the back of her neck, roughly took her mouth, and was rewarded with a gasp.

Jack slipped his tongue between her lips to mimic their earlier fucking. He pushed his way in, sliding his tongue along hers then retreating, assaulting her until she was barely holding herself up, panting from the blast of passion. He made his kiss a wicked promise to her for later.

They came apart as seamlessly as they had come together. Jack watched as she took a step back and straightened her makeshift tunic. "You smell good," he teased, unable to contain his grin. He noticed a blush spread over her skin.

"Stop smelling me," she demanded, her voice pitched and indignant.

"Never." He laughed. "How else would I know when you want me?"

"Maybe you could ask."

He shifted so he was fully facing her, still kneeling but spreading his legs apart, revealing his hard-on. "Do you want to fuck me, Allie?" he asked, laughing. "Because I sure as hell want to fuck you."

He heard an embarrassed moan escape her as she buried her face into her hands, the light from the flashlight bouncing around.

"See? Smelling you saves you from embarrassment." Teasing her was becoming one of his new favorite pastimes. He briefly looked at her stomach again before pushing the uncomfortable thoughts away.

"I do want you again," she confessed, peeking out from her hands to stare at the bulge between his legs.

"Once I finish up here, I'll give myself to you first thing." He winked at her, "You can have your wicked way with me." She dropped her hands and revealed her face. "It's a new deal. I'll be your sexual slave."

Allie laughed softly, "Deal." A pulsing light flashed out from the reactor behind him.

"Watch my back, Allie," he reminded her as he turned back to the job at hand, opening up the holographic keylock, hacking the dated system with ease.

His last conscious sound was of her turning away to watch the darkness as he became a robot, dropping his humanoid half away.

Chapter Twelve:

. . . .

Allie was shivering with desire again. The promise of his body was enough to replace years of pent-up loneliness and frustration, evaporating her old fantasies. She knew she needed him more than she wanted to admit. Attachment was a dangerous thing.

She hadn't known it was possible to procreate with Jack and that made her wary. He alluded that Cyborgs could control it and she hoped that he had.

Her emotions had been thrown around like a sandstorm. All of them were jumbled together until she couldn't tell them apart. It made her emotionally and mentally drained; during times like these, where her fear was palpable and her desire fierce, she found herself confused over what feeling belonged to what emotion.

Allie felt her mind would snap under the stress.

Jack's laughter had banished the darkness for a moment, but it crept its way back in around her now that he was gone. And ever since they had left the grave pit, she could feel something following her. The smell lingered – clung to her – and it only got worse with every passing second.

She squeezed the handle of her dagger to reassure herself of its presence.

She waved the flashlight around the exterior of the room, checking every shadow in every corner.

The machine behind her pulsed bright light intermittently. It built up a tempo as the power source grew stronger. She assumed Jack was coaxing it. The noise of the metal clanging around the room was welcome in her mind. The spaces beyond and the pathways after that remained dark, silent, and scary.

From where she stood, there was only one direction to get to Jack but the ship's corridors spider webbed off after the core room, and it was those directions she watched with intensity, moving the beam of light between.

A loud clamor blasted out from behind her, coming from the reactor. Soon after a bright light source that ran along the hallway walls flickered on, bathing the space in a wash of deep red before they flickered back off.

Allie stiffened in place. She could have sworn that she saw a being illuminated when the red light was cast. Frantically, she waved the flashlight around to locate the anomaly but it only lit up a single section at a time. The shadows flooded in whenever her light moved away.

Her heart beat fast, the breath in her lungs held tight, her throat closed up. Fear stopped her from doing anything but maneuvering the light and she was losing the will to do even that. The light was her defense, but it was also the fastest ticket to losing her mind. She desperately did not want to see her fears take a physical form.

Allie's fear made her focus and that focus was suffocating her. She had walked into the bowels of her worst nightmare and she had done it willingly, and for what? Closure? Jack? What had she been thinking?

She never considered herself to be brave; before her arrival here she was a simple, oppressed girl who followed the rules and dictates of the commune. She never stuck out, never brought attention to herself. How did she end up here?

Allie was about to give in to her cowardice when she was stopped, hearing her name whispered in the dark.

"Allieee," a strained wisp came from the gloom beside her. She turned toward the sound and lifted her light.

Nothing was there but a darkened pathway that led into nothingness.

"Aaalliee," her name came again, slithering through the air. She looked down the path, contemplating her next move when the darkness spoke again.

"I need you." It was fainter now as if it was moving away from her.

"Who are you?" The breath she held for the past minute was released. She waited for an answer that never came. "Hello?" She moved the light around the room again.

Ghosts.

Just then the red neon glow of the ship flickered back on and the machine behind her shook. When it stayed on, not immediately flickering off, she was able to look around and upon first glance, everything was as it should be.

Metal flakes from the deteriorated wall crunched under her feet, the machinery lay in ruins around her. Allie looked up at the pathway where her name had come from and froze.

The low red dim stretched far out before her to the end of the corridor and at the end of the tubular metal hallway was a black ghostly figure, suspended in air. It was far away and blurred all detail but she knew that it was stagnant and staring in her direction. It had long flowing black hair that stuck to the shadows like sludge.

"Allie," a breathy, dull whisper washed over her again. It filled her nostrils with rot.

"Who are you?" She whispered back as if she was next to the wraith.

"You left me here..." the sound hung in the air between them.

"Ophelia?" Allie felt her heart break open, she knew, tears forming in her eyes. It was her, her friend Ophelia, a young female like herself. Ophelia was chosen to be the mate to the usurper Warlord's closest General.

When Allie had first met her soon after arriving at the female commune, she had been a simpering, naive girl who had been excited to pair with a Trentian male. Nobody liked being near her, shadows followed her around, and she was often caught talking to herself and sleepwalking at night.

Nobody liked me either.

"My male is out there right now, fighting for the right to my body, for the future children we will create together." She remembered Ophelia sighing longingly.

She also cried but unlike me, her virgin blood was dripping down her legs. I couldn't save her.

Ophelia told her afterward that the Warlord's best General went straight for her and licked off her tears. He had told her she was pretty when she cried and that she was special to lose her innocence to the Warlord's hand, that he would finish the job during the ceremony the following day in support of his Usurper's celebration.

Allie shook her head. Something happened, a strange, obscure darkness followed the event. Her mind hurt to think about it like she had blocked out the trauma.

The man I was supposed to mate with brutalized my best friend.

Each girl that day had similar, horrifying stories, and it was then that they decided as a group, pressured by Ophelia, to escape before the claimings. Ophelia said she had a plan, that she had made a deal to ensure they would escape successfully to the port, and that a pilot would smuggle them off of the planet.

Allie never got the chance to ask her friend how she managed that feat, but her friend got their group into space and for a short time they were free.

She stared at the phantom, her friend, as it stared right back at her. The only break between them was the noise of the reactor powering up the ship. The red light in the hallway flickered as the dark figure turned away and moved into a room and out of her sight.

She knew this was why she had come back, why she had ended up back here. It was her unfinished business with her friend. The girl who had picked her up and dragged her out of the commune. The girl who had saved her life only to end it here, on this rotten planet.

The two of them had been inseparable for years, ever since Ophelia was delivered to the commune after her testing. They had bonded instantly. Allie, the Earthian bastard, and Ophelia, the crazy half-breed girl who talked to herself. They had both been different, both struggling, and they had found each other.

Tears fell down her cheeks. She couldn't let her go; Allie knew she needed to see this to the end or she would only be a husk of the person she truly could be.

Ophelia has been here all this time.

She looked back at where Jack was working, saying a silent goodbye and a sad, desperate *thank you* in case she was unable to return. Her gaze lingered in his direction, her heart screaming at her to stay with him, to go to his side, but her guilt urged her away.

Her choice was solidified when the ship jerked around her, the ground shaking abruptly then stopping as if to nudge her on. The lights around her quivered.

Without needing another sign, she started down the passage where her friend had just been, making her way carefully over the sharp edges of debris scattered over the ground. She kept her light facing forward to keep her path in sight. The thought of the drifting ghost appearing in front of her scared her out of her mind.

But the thought that the ghost was her friend kept her moving onward and that it was *her* turn to come through for her.

It didn't take long to reach the end of the passageway where she had seen the wraith. Allie didn't know what to expect, but standing where it had been minutes before made her spine tingle with fear. She was dealing with forces that she couldn't understand.

Moving the light to the room where it had disappeared, she illuminated the space, searching for the entity. The red lights only extended to the passageways, leaving the rooms that split off still dark. The space was large; it looked like it had been a meeting place at one point. At one end, she observed what looked like a table shattered against the wall.

It must have slammed into the wall on impact. The only other entrance to the chamber was in the opposite corner from her.

"Hello?" she whispered to the ship again. Receiving only silence in return, she walked into the room.

Allie steadily moved deeper into the ship. Nothing else called out to her and the only sounds that accompanied her were the groans of the ship. The way forward was unusually clear and straightforward. There was only one way to go, as the other pathways were blocked by rubble.

She knew that the entity would keep her on the right path. Allie had a sinking, bottomless feeling in her gut.

The ship violently shook around her, the floor lifting up and then crashing back down. She lost her footing from the heave and dropped to her knees. Something sharp sliced into them.

She yelped as she tried to stand up, reaching down with a wince, finding small glass shards lodged into her skin. Allie pulled out several of the pieces, her fingers coming away with blood. It seeped down her bare legs and smeared over her hands.

The ship shook again soon after but she was prepared for it, balancing with her feet apart. She could hear large crashes behind her as if the interior were falling apart. Scared, she turned around to investigate and discovered that the way back was partially blocked, the ceiling having caved in. Large pipes had dropped down to block her exit.

Allie felt trapped and for a moment wanted to dig her way out and back to Jack.

Did I make the right choice? She reached out to manhandle the metal cylinders out of the way.

"Please help," a sad moan punctuated the space. She turned away from the makeshift jail bars that severed her path to Jack.

"Ophelia?" She flashed the light around, the sound had been right behind her. Hardening herself upon seeing nothing, she moved further into the ship, leaving the pipes behind.

The temperature was dropping with each step she took further into the ship. The sounds of the reactor were now a faint, faraway whisper. She shivered, holding her arms around her frame. Allie could see her breath frosted in the air and she was grateful for the cloak draped around her. The blood on her knees cracked with her every movement, already chilled and dried to her skin.

She was as cold on the outside as she was numb with fear on the inside, fighting herself with every step to not turn back and run to Jack, but every time her doubts began to win over, her friend's voice filled her mind, beckoning her on.

Allie was at a part of the ship that she had never been before. She periodically came across human remains the deeper she traveled, bones of the bodies she could not get to long ago.

The spaces around her looked less like operating rooms and more like storage units, small odd closets and rooms dotted along the exteriors of the large rooms she moved through. In one room, she peeked in and saw a dilapidated bed and rusty bedspring.

Maybe this was where the crew was housed.

She felt a breeze brush past her arm; she jerked it away and stumbled back in trepidation, searching the area for her friend.

She backed up against the wall and trembled, faint from adrenaline and confusion. She stayed like that for a short time before she found the willpower to scan the area with her light again, her hand shaking from the effort. "Ophelia," she breathed. "Where are you?" All she could see around her were the series of doors that led into the smaller living spaces.

Her call was answered.

Her heart stopped.

Straight across from her, the wraith descended down from the shadows above, its hair falling forward as if dripping with black ooze and shade, the face distorted behind it.

"Allie," the entity groaned. It dropped down with a thunk, materializing before her eyes, pooling into an unnatural shape on the ground. "We want you," the thing wailed, its voice overlain with dozens of other voices. The ghost wasn't her friend but a mass of lost souls.

Allie stood there in terror, drowning in the stench of musty soil and death. Her mouth and lungs filled with the putrid scent, the taste adhered to her tongue. She pressed her back into the wall as if she could become one with it.

"Ophelia, are you there?" She asked so softly that she couldn't hear the sound leave her lips.

The wraith vibrated with otherworldly laughter, the cacophony hurting her ears. She watched as the evil faded in and out, there one moment and gone the next, flickering like the lights strewn along the walls outside the armored core. Every time it reappeared, with each quiver, it was closer to her.

The sludge-like hair was branching out around her, pulling from the darkness and yet still clinging to the ghost. Pale, long skeletal arms appeared before it from the muck, clawing at the ground.

She couldn't move as the thing moved its way closer. Allie frantically searched its ever-shifting form for an image of her friend. It was an unearthly malformation of bodies, and it reeked of hatred.

It wanted her, had always wanted her. Searching the planet with its darkness every night for years to haunt her.

Allie's arm felt like lead but she lifted it anyway to beam the light directly at it. Any resemblance to her friend vanished as the faces shifted into the other girls who had been on the ship with them that had died. Their voices sounded as one, the groans leaking out of its mouth were abominable, the jaw stretched down, revealing an endless black void. It crept closer to her.

She focused on the horror of what was before her, knowing that she should have been a part of the mass of lost souls creeping closer, but she had miraculously survived, escaped the fate of an undying trauma. The pain of having hope firmly in your grasp and then having it forcefully taken away.

The souls of the girls before her were not the same ones she had grown up with, but a macabre mass of angry, painful emotions that had settled in and rotted in a place from which there was no escape. They were tied to the ship.

An electric crackle ghosted her body.

Where could souls go when they were so far out in the fringes of space? They had been left here like discards to suffer alone.

Allie didn't want the same fate.

She pushed her back along the chilled wall, putting more space between her and the suffering mass. It was moving slowly, the decayed arms dragging its heavy, wet body over the floor, weighed down by its physical form.

Allie felt the darkness creep its way around her body to caress her skin.

She didn't dare blink, her eyes dried out from the watching the oncoming mass move closer. When she felt her back hit the corner of the large central room, she pushed her way up, feeling the pain in her knees, the little pieces of glass still lodged in her skin, making each movement a cringing effort. The shards chafed her skin tissue.

The groans of the mass filling the room made her ears bleed, and a sharp pain formed behind her eyes.

She slid her back around the outer edges, keeping her light directed at the thing slowly making its way toward her as she made her way back to the exit. When she was only several agonizing steps away from her destination, the wails vanished and the darkness swirling around her loosened up. The oppressive thickness around her moved away.

The mass of souls had stopped, suspended in space, the physical form vibrating. It was no longer moving; the only movement now was her erratic pulse.

Allie stood there, slightly hunched over in pain, her body propped up at an angle against the cold metal wall, facing the fate she had escaped when a familiar faint scratch sounded the air above her.

It was so quiet now that anyone else had to concentrate to hear it, but for her, it was as loud as thunder in her ears.

Once again she couldn't bring herself to move, the fear she had felt morphing to despair and morphing again into terror because Allie *knew* that scratching, she knew what caused it and it wasn't the grudge crawling before her. It was something from the abyss, an evil that had no right to be on her plane of existence.

The scratching stopped, and her heart skipped a beat as something wet and warm dripped onto her face. The strange sensation pulled her back to the reality of the situation around her. She reached up to wipe the drip off of her face when another one fell, smearing down her cheek.

She looked up slowly and gazed into the face of her nightmares.

Her eyes were filled with a wide, twisted grin engorged with sharp, discolored teeth. The mouth around it blackened out before it melded into a pasty, pale, inhuman face. The eyes glaring down at her were gaping dead hollows.

The creature was on the ceiling, leering at her, so close that she could smell the stale death on its breath. Its breath tickled loose strands of her hair as her mouth fell open into a scream that she never released.

The next moment she was slammed to the ground by the large force. Long jagged nails clawed at her body as she felt slimy, loose skin slide over her legs when a sharp pain stunned her as something sliced the skin on her upper arm.

She felt faint from the burst of pain but her adrenaline went into overdrive and kept her from fainting.

The beast was snapping at her, aiming for her throat while simultaneously trying to pin her down. She knocked her flashlight hard into the side of its head, losing her grip on her first defense; her hand came away with strands of grimy hair.

Allie heard her flashlight fall and roll away from her. She kicked her legs out, pressing her glass ravaged knees into the creature's body. When she made contact, the thing howled out a shriek and slammed its clawed fist into her stomach.

She felt the abrupt loss of air as she wheezed, the shock of her sudden loss of breath paralyzed her for an agonizing moment. A painful yank snapped her head as it grabbed her hair, pulling it up with enough force to expose her throat.

Allie pushed with every muscle in her body, her lost scream from earlier filling the room as she bore her entire body to the side, feeling the abomination above her shift and slide to the side. Its probing nails sliced her skin little, jagged nicks.

The ship heaved heavily, lifting upward, lodging the room at a sharp angle. The beast lost its hold on her hair and flew across the room with a monstrous scream. A loud, high-pitched wail from their observer joined in the symphony.

Allie struggled on the floor, grabbing at anything that would stop her slide down the room toward the thing now clawing its way back to her on the other end. She saw the exit begin to pass her by; she threw her leg out to catch the side, halting her descent.

With her free hand, she seized the door panel and hauled herself through. The ship trembled around her, slamming back down. She could feel a sucking sensation around her as the ship dipped further into the ground.

On heavy legs she stood up, using the wall as support, her hand streaking blood as it moved. Every fiber of her being screamed at her to stop and collapse and give up, but she refused to listen.

I would lose everything if I died on this ship. She could hear the scratches start up behind her.

Without another thought, she started running. The ship was so dark that she found herself tripping over debris and running into the dark metal walls, all the while hearing the ever-familiar scratches behind her. Far in the background, almost lost over the thing pursuing her, she heard the loud pitiful cries of the souls left behind.

Her eyes welled up for their pain. *I pray they find peace.* The cries came to a stop as if they heard her thoughts.

Her foot caught on a loose metal plate, twisting her ankle. She fell forward, from the shock when her head was thrown violently back again; the beast had caught up to her.

In the distance before her, she could see a pulsing red light indicating the passageways leading back to the reactor. *I'm so close.* She felt the familiar claws sink into her twisted foot as she stared at the lights.

Jack was right there.

Furious, her agony flooded out of her body as she saw her chance at freedom being denied again. She kicked her leg out with all her might, thrusting the thing sideways. She turned around to face it.

Allie clenched her hand, remembering the dagger that she still held, having forgotten it with her fixation on the flashlight.

She propelled forward at the monster that was now trying to bite down on her calf and brought the dagger down, feeling it slide into wet flesh. The thing screeched and tried to slither back into the shadows beyond, but she wouldn't let it, bringing the dagger down again, stopping its movements.

Her mind was overwhelmed with bloodlust, stabbing at the abomination over and over, the blood and carnage splattering away.

"He told me to stab until it's dead!" she shrieked, knowing the ghoul beneath her had perished some time ago. She was unable to stop.

Chapter Thirteen:

. . . .

Jack carefully pulled the last of the wires out, keeping one hand firmly in place to retain his connection to the reactor. He was temporarily acting as a conduit for the large machine. The electrical pulses were his only lead to the working circuitry.

He was part of the ship at that moment, feeling the energy flow through him and release, simultaneously powering up the core while it charged up his robotics.

He felt invigorated.

The ship groaned beneath him, the floor heaving sideways as if something had hit the side of the ship. Jack lost his connection to the core as his body was thrown to the side. His hand reactively went to the circuits he had already harvested that were now strapped to his thigh, ensuring that they were intact and undamaged.

The reactor convulsed, and he watched as it rapidly lost power now that he was no longer maintaining his connection to it. It was going to die – the pulsing lights had longer intervals between them as the piece of deteriorating metal depleted its remaining power.

He called out, "Allie, are you okay?" Jack stood up while he scanned the area for her presence. The ship shook again, the movements progressively becoming more violent. His internal alert systems sprang back to life, overwhelming him with screams of danger.

Fuck, where is she? He picked up the pace.

His hand shot out to the barrier, keeping his feet steady as the ship jerked downward and a feeling of vertigo encompassed him.

Jack sensed several wurms just outside the battle cruiser, ramming their bodies into it. *Fuck.* He screamed several curses to himself. *How did they get through the rocky, mountainous crust?* The magnetic field and the electrical pulses must be drawing them like moths to the flame. *They're trying to destroy the ship.*

He ducked under the barrier. "Allie, we need to go! Now!" he shouted, realizing it fell on deaf ears. She wasn't there.

Giant metal panels dislodged and crashed around him; the interior was crumbling to pieces with each impact. He searched for the girl as he ran to his half-buried pack and pulled it free, slinging it on, scanning the ship's rapidly changing interior. In the distance, coming from outside the ship, he heard a loud monstrous roar as a wurm broke through the surface; the ground quaked when its giant body hit the dirt.

The potent, magnetic field was screwing with his processing and concentration. He could sense life-forms, but he had a hard time pinpointing their location. "Allie!" He yelled louder into the space, deciding to track her the primitive way, picking up the direction her scent was the freshest; he followed it down a decrepit pathway that was now partially destroyed by the barrage of violence.

Where is she? Why didn't she stay near me?

Everything in him screamed to cut his losses and get out. His thoughts felt like the pulsing red lights of the reactor but at a much higher, more stressful tempo. He pushed them away; he wasn't going to leave without the girl.

Jack dodged as a metal pipe broke away and flung outward, nearly smashing into the side of his head. The girl's scent was stronger the farther he went, and became almost overpowering when he caught the fresh scent of blood.

Her blood.

He balanced his body as he rounded the corner, veering off into a side room where her blood was stronger and fresher. He looked around frantically, but she was still nowhere in sight. In the center, he knelt down where glass shards lay strewn about, scattered to every corner of the room from the tremors. Pieces of them were coated in her blood.

He picked one up and examined it before tossing it away. It wasn't a significant amount.

A different smell permeated the air as he quietly stood back up and rescanned the immediate area, with no effect. It smelled like soil, and not just any soil, but the moist swamplands back on Earth. It smelled like musk and decay and the acrid odor that floats in the air after a bloody battle.

Jack sensed that he was no longer alone as a loud sobbing wail vibrated through the thick metal walls around him. The sound came from somewhere deep in the ship, the vibrations were faint ripples. It was like a hundred beings crying all at once. The sound stung his ears.

He unsheathed his pistol and cocked it while he quietly proceeded further, the smell of carnage growing stronger as did the volume of the crying. He focused on the small communicator he had given Allie days prior but could not locate its signal. He gave up with a frustrated groan.

It was then that, when he strained his ears, he heard Allie's voice. "–to stab until it's dead!" she shrieked in a frantic curse.

Jack rounded the corner, following her voice, and froze.

The girl was on her knees, stabbing the ever-living crap out of something beneath her. Her body glowed like a bright red beacon in his infrared vision. Neon red was sprayed over the floor and walls around her.

"Allie?" He walked up behind her, staring down at the floor. When he rounded her body and stood in front of her, he could see what she was aggressively destroying: the creepy thing from the cave.

Her eyes were wild, and parts of her hair were plastered to her face and body, soaked with blood and sweat. Jack stood there and watched as she relentlessly stabbed at the thing before her – as if she were in a trance. He would have gotten lost in that strange moment if the ship hadn't begun to shake again, bringing him back to the danger of their situation.

He knelt before her and sheathed his gun, using his free hand to swipe the hair off of her face before cupping her cheeks.

Tears were flowing from her eyes, creating clear streaks down her blood-encrusted face. Allie wasn't a celestial angel crying bloody tears, but a bloody angel crying tears of pain.

"Sweetheart, you're okay. You did good. It's dead." He watched as her movements faltered as she looked at him, registering the scene around her, the glaze in her eyes clearing.

"Jack?" she asked hesitantly.

"Yeah, it's me, baby. You did great but now we need to go." The weapon she held dropped from her hand. The sides now dulled, the tip blunted and dripping with gore.

"We need to go," she repeated him.

"Yes, it's not safe here." He moved his hands to her fore-arms and pulled her up to a standing position until she yelped, crumpling back to the ground.

"My ankle–my leg, it's broken." She cried. He ran his hand over the area, feeling the fracture in her tibia under his fingers.

"All right, put your arms around my neck and your legs around my waist," he said as he lifted her into his arms. She complied with a whimper. "Hold tight, Allie, I'm going to get us out of here." Jack lifted her thigh on his left side higher up so she wouldn't get chafed by the circuits and they wouldn't be damaged.

He looked down at the mangled carcass on the floor beside his feet, pleased that there was no trace of its creepy smile; in fact, there was no face left at all. He gave the girl a gentle squeeze as he quickened his pace into a run towards the surface.

The ship was falling apart around them. It took all of his effort to monitor the environment, focus on their escape, and carry all of his precious cargo. The frequencies were still inter-fering with his internal processing system. He barely had time to register the shifts of metal before they fell around him, stop-ping before loose pipes slammed into them moments before they cracked open and splintered.

He kept one arm firmly around Allie, keeping her body pinned and protected from the destruction raining down around them. He could sense her breathing begin to even out as she came down from her frenzy.

There were several behemoths outside the wreckage, swim-ming around, aggressive and enraged by the electric currents. He knew more were on their way, sensing several breaking their way through the mountain, forcing their way into an area they otherwise would have avoided. This place was a deathtrap.

Jack felt a wave of violence course through him, willing him to stay, to reap destruction alongside the wurms. *This* was what he was created for. Battle. War. His body was alive from the reactor and the power outside was beckoning him to join the fray.

The whimper of the girl in his arms brought him back down.

The exit before him was blocked by rubble that buried the long passageway they had used to enter the ship. A wurm ran its body into the side of the hull at that moment, making the ship shift forward, sinking even further into the sand.

The ground slurped it up hungrily, actively trying to rid the planet of the invasive machine that had invaded its world. The planet was riding itself of the thorn in its side.

Without stopping, Jack ran full speed at the damaged exterior wall, pushing his arm out to shield the girl from the impact. The wall caved outward from the contact; he quickly set his hand on it and transferred all of his remaining bots to destroy the wall.

A ray of sun shot through, illuminating the dreary interior, brightening their forms and making their blood-drenched clothes glow. The girl lifted her head away from his neck and looked out. With his hand still positioned on the deteriorating wall, Jack leaned down and kissed her forehead.

"See, we're almost out," he breathed over her skin.

He pounded at the ruined metal with his hand, breaking it apart, letting more of the sunlight through. Looking out himself, he saw the wurms slither right below the surface, the spikes along their backs feathering the sand. The entire pit was now a funnel and they were right in the center. The ground was approaching fast as the ship lurched downward.

The scene reminded him of shark-infested waters.

Jack knew if they didn't leave now they were going to be sucked up along with the ship.

"Hold tight. I've got you, but I need you to not let go. This won't be easy." He waited for her acknowledgment.

"I won't let go." She buried her face back into his neck.

He kicked the crumbling wall now that it was brittle enough for them to push their way through. He snaked both his arms around the girl's body and backed up, creating enough space to build the right momentum and, just as the ship jerked, he ran forward and jumped through the hole.

The last thing he heard from the ship was a distant sad cry, buried by its fate.

The landing brought him to his knees, his legs sinking into the unpacked sand. He got up and started running as soon as he knew he was clear of the waterfall of dirt pulling everything down. Every step was a fight to keep them out of the inner ring of the giant funnel.

This day is not going as I planned. He groaned from the effort and the loss of all of his nanobots.

The exertion it took for him to fight against the sinkhole behind him was monumental, even for his superior endurance. *It's nice to be challenged.* He thought to himself. *Just not while I have a dying girl in my arms.*

The ever-present wurms swam around the pit, sometimes emerging upwards to ram their lengths into the battle cruiser, forcefully trying to obliterate its existence. Fortunately for them, most of the monsters were lurking deep underground, working on the parts that had been buried some time ago. Now that he had full function of all of his cyberbotics and processing units he could sense the wurms tearing the metal to shreds, leaving nothing behind.

For once he felt a real spark of luck – it was incredible that he and Allie had escaped the mausoleum. If he had been fully human, they would have both been dead by now. But then again, he would never have come here for parts to repair his ship, instead opting to take the safer route of sending out a distress signal throughout the sector.

Jack felt the girl in his arms fading fast and he could tell that her body was about to crash.

If she doesn't pass out soon, she may go into shock.

He knew that she was coming down from the high of hysteria, the blood coating her body a clear indication that she had been hurt. He had to get them both someplace safe and he had to do it soon.

His attention shifted back to the events around him, noticing that a wurm was heading in their direction and it was going to emerge at any moment right beneath them.

He rolled to the side at the last second, cradling the girl as the giant head broke through the ground and landed directly on the disappearing ship, smashing it down. By the time the wurm began to burrow back into the ground, the battle cruiser was gone, devoured by the planet.

The whimper against his chest set him to moving again; he rolled onto his knees and stood up, continuing his ascent out of the now quiet pit. He adjusted his pack as he climbed.

Soon after they reached the top and the sand gave way to the rocky, mountainous landscape. He breathed a sigh of relief. They were finally out of immediate danger and now he just had to find someplace safe to break for the girl. Blood now drenched the both of them.

Some of her wounds must be deep if they haven't clotted yet. She was losing a significant amount of blood.

"It's okay, sweetheart, you're going to be all right," he relayed with a confidence that he was having a hard time believing.

So he ran and ran until they had long since passed their camp from the previous night. He stopped shortly to pour water down her throat but then continued on. He wanted to get as far away from the nightmare as possible so that when he set Allie down, he could reassure her it was now a distant memory.

The afternoon crested and moved toward evening before he actively sought a place for them to rest. The place he scouted wasn't great but it would work as he inspected a small tunnel that led into the mountain, the walls carved out by the bones of a long dead wurm.

Jack shrugged off the pack and delicately laid Allie down. When she was curled up on the ground, a small, sad moan escaped her lips. He felt guilt, pain, and anger that he hadn't been aware enough to stop her foolish descent into the ship.

When she was on her way to recovery, he was going to demand answers.

He turned back to the pack and emptied it, taking out the blankets, laying them out and folding them over to create a small cushion. When he was satisfied, he gingerly lifted Allie into a sitting position and unbuckled the clips of her cloak and pulled off her make-shift mesh tunic, both pieces now beyond repair from damage and blood.

Her eyes remained closed the entire time, and he assumed she was struggling to distance her mind from the pain she was feeling.

"Allie? I'm going to need you to stay awake. Just for a short time. I need to check your head for a concussion." He kept his voice soft yet stern and authoritative.

"Jack?" she breathed.

"Yes, sweetheart?" He leaned over her, pulling her hair away from her body at the same time.

"I'm sorry," she whimpered, tears forming in her eyes.

"You should be sorry. You lied to me and then did something stupid." He ground out, "But I'm sorry too, I promised you that you wouldn't get hurt and you did. So we both didn't live up to our word." He turned away to start a large fire, one that would last the night and keep their camp well lit.

I'm fucking done with this planet and its weird creatures and heavy darkness.

"I always hurt my friends. I knew what was on that ship and I let you go anyway. I thought I could protect you from its evil and I not only left you but I broke my promise and almost got myself killed." She continued in tears, "I left to get answers and I got them. My friend wasn't there but I left you too. I wasn't watching your back." She stumbled over her words.

Jack was stuck between wanting to comfort her and wanting to lay out the hard truth. He knew she was strong enough to be treated like a soldier, but she was also dealing with a trauma that he couldn't understand. He decided on neither method.

"First off, we're not friends. Friends don't fuck each other. Second, you're going to heal up and get through this because we have a deal, a contract, and I hate when people try and renege on their word. So I am going to help you recover, but I'm not going to do the recovering for you. That's up to you." He softened his voice, "I saw what you did back on the ship to that nasty smiley shit and I'm proud of you. You listened to me and aimed to kill. I'm also inappropriately hard right now because it was the sexiest sight I have ever seen." He took the cleaning fabric he had pulled from his pack and started to glide it over her damaged form. The debris that was plastered to her hands vanishing before she took the cloth from him, wiping at her face and arms.

A small twitch played on her lips, "Of course you would say that."

He got the smile he wanted to see out of her and Jack knew now that whatever happened next, she would overcome this. He grinned back down at her.

He reached up and rubbed her scalp, feeling nor sensing any bumps or bruises. "Your head is fine. You can drift off to sleep if you want to." He leaned back to unbuckle his body armor, peeling it and his weapons off of his body. He then carefully removed the circuit boards and placed them in his pack for the night.

"Jack, if we're not friends, what are we then?" the girl asked him tiredly, wincing from her movements to face him.

He went back to her side and helped her sit up and it was when her fingers darted to her knees that he saw tiny flakes of glass lodged in her skin. "Stop." He stilled her hand and fumbled with his medical supplies, pulling out a syringe filled with pain relief and a disc of medicinal salve before he answered her question.

"We're currently business partners, we're also partners in crimes against this planet," he grinned as he injected her. "We're lovers, we're two beings who are alone, stranded on a planet billions of miles away from civilization, who got dealt shitty cards." Jack finished as he took out his tweezers and pulled the tiny slivers out of her skin, spreading the salve over each area afterward.

She watched him with curiosity, wincing in pain now and again. Luckily the painkiller he gave her was strong enough to numb her out once it spread through her bloodstream.

"I like that," she smiled. "I've never had those relationships before. It feels like a fresh start – I never want to have a friend again."

He wanted to laugh as her expression went soft, her eyes widening as the painkiller went into effect. "Well, I don't have many friends but the ones I do have I keep at a distance. You can't hurt what you don't have. I understand." He leaned forward and kissed her, aware that she was naked in front of him. His tongue slid over her lips because her mouth tasted like tears.

He lifted her up while his mouth still explored hers hungrily and laid her down on the blankets. "You need to sleep now. It will help you heal faster." He said against her lips before pulling away. "I'm going to stitch up your calf and your arm and apply the serum to your cuts while you're out." Jack watched as she closed her eyes before he moved. "When you wake tomorrow, you'll feel better," he promised.

"Thank you, Jack," she whispered sleepily. "Thank you for saving me. Again."

"Shh," he placed one more light kiss on her lips. "Sleep." He waited until she drifted off before he covered her upper body with one of the blankets, then repositioned himself at her feet.

He grabbed the numbing agent and slathered it over her broken ankle as well as the areas around where the creature had torn her open. Jack disinfected each cut and tear before stitching her closed. He repeated the process for her arm.

When he was done cleaning her up and fortifying her wounds, he sat back and took in her injuries, moving himself back to her extremely swollen ankle. He lifted it carefully between his hands with the intent of locating her break. He gently probed her skin with his fingers until they were in position.

Jack knew that she was sleeping and that the painkillers were keeping her that way, but he also knew that she was going to feel it, if not tonight, tomorrow morning. He hoped he had given her long enough to fall under.

He watched her face as he snapped her leg, realigning her bone using his strength to traction her skin. A short pop and the fractured tibia was back in place. Her body spasmed as a pained moan escaped her lips. Jack felt like praying to the stars at that moment because she hadn't woken up from the pain.

I don't want to cause her any more pain. She has already gone through too much.

There was nothing to be done for her bruises or the blood loss this night, tomorrow he would make sure she ate and rehydrated. He moved away from her still form to tend the fire while he refueled himself, giving his body the extra nourishment to enhance his effectiveness at replacing his bots.

When he was finished eating, he threw the wrapper of his protein ration into the flame and addressed his carnage-covered armor, picking the pieces up with disgust and appreciation. Blood soaked through portions of the material and it angered him that it belonged to Allie.

He should have known better than to completely shut down when he was working on the reactor. *Everything happened so quickly and my sensors were being scrambled*, he knew his excuses fell flat and that he had failed in more ways than one that day.

Jack picked up the offending pieces and walked outside their small camp to discard them, feeding them to the hungry wildness of the planet. When he was satisfied that his failures were buried deep he made his way back to the fire and laid himself down next to Allie, tucking her blanket over both of their bodies. He curled his body around hers protectively.

"I will make it up to you," he whispered into the golden gloom.

Now that they were a significant distance from the crash site it was easier for him to monitor their whereabouts with clarity. There was nothing that could damage them for miles in every direction and the only sound in the darkening night was the snap of the fire and Allie's soft breathing.

He buried his face in her wild hair and drifted off to sleep.

Chapter Fourteen:

· · · ·

Allie awoke the next morning to the sound of scraping. She pried her eyes open, her eyelashes crusty from tears, and spotted Jack running a stone over the edge of his dagger. Small silvery sand came away.

She felt hot and weak and it took her a fair amount of effort to move her arm up to prop her torso and head high enough to look down at her body.

"You need to eat." Jack stepped back into view, his voice held a hint of anger as he approached her with a ration of food and a canister. *Eat?* She looked at her foot and felt a wave of nausea wash through her. Her weakened state forgotten, she turned to the side and heaved.

Nothing came up but the sounds of hacking. She felt a tug on her hair as it was pulled back from her face.

"You're dehydrated, malnourished, suffering from blood loss, and are coming down from some powerful painkillers." She could feel his steely arm wrap around her back and lift her to a sitting position. Her vision was doing flips, the area around her spinning. It made her want to dry heave again.

His hand cradled her spinning head as a water canister was pushed against her mouth; he tipped it up until she felt liquid touch her tongue. The water soon filled her mouth and streamed down the sides of her chin. The lukewarm liquid slid down her dry throat until it pooled at the bottom of her stomach.

Water had never tasted so heavenly.

"Good." He poured the entire bottle down before tossing it aside while she lifted her hand and wiped the stray drops off of her chin.

"Jack?" She peered at him, her sight continued to spin but was now caught in a cobweb, dragging it along for the ride as she willed her head to be clear of it.

He answered her by pushing a ration between her lips, practically shoving it in her mouth before her reflexes took over and she bit down to stop it from being rammed down her throat. Annoyed, she chewed slowly, feeling her lost energy begin to return. It was only after she worked her way through the bar that she realized that she was still naked, that her only covering was currently pooled in her lap.

She looked around for her clothing but found nothing. *Why does this keep happening to me?* It was becoming much too hot to be wrapped up in a blanket. Feeling herself weaken from the effort of even thinking about it, she lifted the cloth over her breasts.

"You're well on your way to being healed," he said flatly, sitting back and putting space between them.

She stretched her limbs and shifted her form just enough to get a feel of what she would be dealing with; she felt sore all over but none of the sharp pain from yesterday. *Was it yesterday?* The sun was out.

"How long have I been asleep?" Her voice felt weak.

"A little over a day. We left the ship twenty-six Earth hours ago," he answered. "Don't move your arm or your leg quickly or you'll tear the stitches."

Allie tensed her muscles in each area, feeling the toughness of her stitches and the tightness of her skin. She looked at them, barely even seeing the sutures; her skin looked perfectly aligned but for a glossy white line. The main indicator that she was sewn up was the rosy pink of her flesh around the affected areas.

Her eye caught the large bruises that blotched her ankle and lower leg, her foot unrecognizable from the swelling. She reached forward to run her fingers over the delicate skin.

"I realigned your broken bone while you were asleep last night."

"Thank you. It feels sore but not painful." She focused on her knees next, acknowledging that he had removed all the glass from her skin. There was nothing left but patches of pale white flesh. New scars to add to her collection.

"You're welcome." He snapped at her, bringing her focus back to him.

"Is something wrong?"

Once again he didn't answer her, choosing instead to move his attention to her feet. He coated his hands with the medicinal salve and spread it over her legs. She watched as his large hands cupped her calves, lifted her legs, and massaged every square inch of her skin. The tips of his fingers traced the small, shallow slashes that peppered her from toe to knee.

Her breath hitched when he pushed her legs apart, drawing the small blanket upward to bunch at her waist. The entire lower half of her body was exposed to his view. She could feel a heat spread like wildfire through her body.

"I wish you had a cut further up so I didn't have to feel like such an asshole for wanting to touch you." The pads of his fingers ran little circles behind her knees.

She felt so fuzzy, so warm, so weak. Her existence could melt into the ground just from his words. Her body ached in more ways than one and was soft and pliable and receptive to his attention.

There was something dark and powerful about him when he was dressed in his sharp armor. The crossing of buckles that stretched over his straining muscles, the stiff mesh undertone to his metal plating, and the grey unbreakable, unrippable under armor. Except now, large portions of his armor were missing, his chest bare under many of the straps.

Her breath felt strangled as she was unable to suck in air from how much she wanted him. He exuded confidence and control, while at the same time feeling like a violent warning.

It entranced and frightened her when he would appear like a human male one moment, then as a robot the next. He transitioned back and forth in the blink of an eye, when she knew he was focused solely on her and yet aware of everything happening around them. Jack and safety were becoming one and the same. He had given her the push, the opportunity, to face her demons, and then he saved her soul.

He saved it and then took it for himself. She wanted to be one of the many swimming in his stormy eyes. She wanted to be the only one.

When she lowered her body to lie back down on the folded blanket, he moved his fingers up past her knees. Goosebumps prickled her skin and her existence was defined by them and his fingers.

Jack was staring between her legs with furious intensity. His fingers became his hands and they became restraints. The cords in his neck stiffened as she stared back at him, his jaw ticked. Her goosebumps faded and warm waves of embarrassment took its place the longer he held her, staring at her. She shifted to push the blanket down.

He caught her hands and lifted his gaze, locking eye contact with her. "Why did you leave me?" His voice was laced with menace.

Allie took a shaky breath as she tried to pull her hands free from his grip. She closed her eyes to break the intensity and the cobwebs that still remained.

"I heard my friend and I saw something. I thought it was her and I needed to face her," she said softly, wishing she could just forget the events of yesterday.

"You could have said something, warned me."

"I thought about it, once or twice, I wanted to, but the despair in its voice." She shivered, "She saved my life and I left her there on that evil ship to rot. They were all rotting and there was nothing I could do." A tear fell from her eye to slide off and land somewhere in her tangled hair. "I took the light and your dagger with me."

"You could have been killed. I told you– from the first day– that I don't do search and rescue and you nearly died." He let go of her hands abruptly and threw the blanket off her. "Look at your body, you had half a hundred cuts, you're covered in bruises, you've been bitten through muscle tissue, you have a broken tibia, and that's probably nothing compared to your mental state."

Allie pushed herself back up, angry at his words. "I'm alive and I'm healing, both because of you. I did not expect either from you, I know you don't do search and rescue. I'm not one to easily forget. I left you and I don't regret it." She was gaining energy from her anger.

"Why don't you regret it?" he asked, his voice low as he reached out to take a lock of her hair between his fingers.

"She wasn't there." Allie looked down at her hands.

"Your friend?"

"Yes," she sighed. "I know now, I never left her."

"How are you so certain?" The tug on her hair made her scalp tingle.

"I never felt her presence, at least not the *real* her. It's hard to explain, and I don't think you would believe me even if I tried."

"I believe there was something wrong with that ship. I believe that she wasn't there. The ship was, how should I say this, wrong? I'm also having a tough time with explanations today."

"You believe me?" She wrapped her hand around the one tugging her hair.

"What happened may be unexplainable but yes, I believe you."

Allie felt a sense of relief overcome her; she wasn't crazy. "Thank you, Jack, I can't tell you how much that means to me. I thought I was crazy. I thought I had finally cracked."

The corner of his lip lifted up in a smile. "If you're cracked, that makes you all the more perfect." He leaned forward and brushed his lips over hers. The kiss so light it could have been made of steam and whispers. She felt herself crack a little more when he drew away.

"You need to rest more. The energy your body needs to heal will deplete faster if you remain awake." His hands moved over her shoulders and lightly pushed her back down. Her body once again lay on the blankets.

"You'll be here when I wake up?" A wave of soul-deep exhaustion settled in her bones. Her eyes, once easy to keep open when sitting up, now felt like they were holding the weight of the world. Even if he told her he was leaving she didn't think she could muster enough strength to stop him.

"I'll be here. You won't be able to walk by yourself for some time until your foot has had time to mend. The swelling hasn't gone down, but it will once we're back at my ship and we can ice it." Jack tucked the blanket comfortably back around her. The heat from earlier was only a minor nuisance now that she was exhausted and reassured.

"I can stay here and heal if you want to go back to your ship. I still have my rations, so would just need some water. Once my foot is good enough to stand on I can meet you back at your ship in a few days."

His eyes flared. "You're not alone anymore, Allie. I may still seem like a stranger to you but by now I would have hoped that you knew me better, after everything."

"That's–" He cut her off before she could respond.

"Tomorrow I'll carry you back. We'll be at our destination by nightfall. There is nothing you can do about it, I'll overpower you if you attempt to deviate from my plans. There is no place you can hide from me." She watched his face go from angry to threatening.

"I didn't mean–"

"I don't give a fuck what you meant. Go to sleep." He walked out of the cave.

• • • •

ALLIE WAS GOING TO faint. She had woken the next morning by being lifted off the ground and cradled in Jack's arms.

They had barely spoken all day, only stopping at short intervals so she could relieve herself and eat and drink. The tension from the prior evening was still sharp.

She tried to keep her eyes closed all day as the speed he was moving was making her dizzy. Each jostle of every step he took resounded through her body. Allie knew he was angry but she didn't know how to fix it. All she wanted was this ordeal to be over with. She needed time to think, to be alone, and to regain some measure of control over her situation.

It was just after nightfall when they approached the surrounding terrain of her cave. The familiar landmarks beckoned like beacons of home as her ache morphed into muddy relief. She could relax once she was in her own space. The thought of sinking into her spring and wiggling her toes to the glowing blue entities beneath could be a dream come true.

It wasn't until a little time later that she realized that he was moving through the terrain and past her home, that they were still heading toward his ship. It wasn't a comfortable feeling going into his space, but a feeling filled with trepidation and anxiety. Any control that she had left would be taken away once they entered the hatch.

"Jack? Could you take me back to my cave tonight?"

He looked down at her and continued to move forward. "No. I want to get you into my medical bay and make sure you're on the mend."

"I feel fine. The only ache I have now is in my foot and some tightness where the stitches are. I would really like to go home." She was willing to beg, every step took her further from where she wanted to be and closer to his destination.

"Let me get you checked over and then if you still want to, I will take you back to your cave."

"It's almost fully dark now." The tremors of the wurms moving below them increased with every step.

"It's not a problem for me to move around after dark."

His grip tightened around her when a rather volatile quake hit them. "I don't want you traveling after dark. Just take me back now and I can go to your medical bay tomorrow." She was willing him with her mind to listen to her. *Take me back!*

"Worried about me?" He smirked and kept moving forward. She stretched her neck and looked behind them longingly, knowing her imaginary mind powers sucked. He wasn't going to take her home until he got what he wanted.

"Of course I would be worried about you. It's dangerous at night, especially in the dark. You know that." She sighed, deflated and focused on him instead.

He laughed, startling her. "What?" she asked.

"It's cute that you would worry about me. It's downright adorable. I'm a difficult being to kill, or even hurt for that matter." He squeezed her briefly in a hug. "I should give you information about my kind when we get back." He leaned over and buried his face into her hair. "I like that you would be worried about me."

She liked it when he was in a good mood – she'll worry about him more often. It was infectious and made her feel better about being in his space ship tonight now that his grumpiness had gone away.

"I'll stay the night," she conceded.

"I know. I really wasn't going to give you a choice."

Allie sighed as the last ray of light washed over them and then vanished beyond the horizon. The night sky was now prominently above them with billions of twinkling stars gazing down at their moving forms. She felt at peace looking up at them, and the starlight made the normally brown-gold planet into a deep blue-grey. Her home was beautiful when it wanted to be. Beautiful and wild.

"Finally."

Her attention was brought back to Jack, he was looking ahead as he quickened his pace into a jog, his ship now in sight far in the distance.

A little while later they were crossing through the hatch and into the large circular room with the holographic floating planet.

She was set down on one of the chairs in the middle while he dropped his pack to the floor with a loud thunk, the metal plates attached to it slamming together.

She was still only wearing the blanket from the night before wrapped tightly around her chest and tucked in at her shoulder. It was uncomfortable and she hoped she would be rid of it soon.

The ship was just as it was before, stark but still a welcomed sight. The purity and crispness of the design were the exact opposite of the destroyed battle cruiser. It was everything this planet was now and it gave her a sense of security in knowing that it would be a temporary escape.

Tonight will be okay. It's safe here. It's safe with Jack.

Allie watched Jack fiddle with a translucent screen on the wall. He was typing in a series of numbers while his other hand was placed on another, different pad. The ship soon after powered on with a quiet hum, the low lights on the floor replaced with brighter white lights.

"The ship is on standby. It shouldn't attract unwanted attention from the wurms. There are no electrical or magnetic pulses coming from it. It's powered by stored energy for now." He looked over at her, "We'll be safe." The translucent screen vanished but his hand remained on the pad. A moment later a wall opened up to reveal a small stark room. "The medical bay. It rarely gets used," he answered before she could ask.

He walked back to her side and lifted her in his arms walking over to a cushioned white bed that extended from the wall from inside the bay and placed her on it gently.

"Will this hurt?" she asked, watching him turn his back to her. A clear glass frame appeared out of nowhere and covered over the bed and her, trapping her inside.

"No."

Her hand instinctively pushed at the enclosure, feeling an abrupt sense of entrapment. "What's happening?" She wanted out.

"Calm down. I can sense your heart rate increasing. The machine is going to scan you and run some tests, looking for infections, abnormalities, the works. It's going to give you several vaccinations as well." He said as the glass above her vibrated and glowed. A blue light moved over her tense form. To the side, next to Jack, she could see a screen appear on the wall with numbers coursing by. Jack wasn't looking at it but was instead looking at her, his eyes soft yet intense.

A cool spray misted over her skin, sending a shiver through her. It dissipated quickly. She was watching Jack throughout the whole process, unaware of the tiny needles that appeared on the opposite side. Her body jerked when a series of tiny pricks ran down her undamaged arm. It was over before she could move away. She ran her hand down her arm, rubbing away the uncomfortable sensations.

The glass barrier lifted away and vanished into the wall.

Allie sat up and reached for Jack, wrapping her arms around him. She was uncomfortable with the medical bay and needed to feel connected to him again. His arms snaked around her body and lifted her into a tight embrace. "I don't like being in here."

"You'll never have to be in here again if it's up to me, but the medical bay has its uses. I would prefer you healthy and safe than in pain and damaged."

"I don't want to be alone, Jack." She whispered. The last time she was in a medical bay had been an unpleasant experience.

"I'm not going anywhere, sweetheart."

She burrowed as fiercely as she could into his hard form.

His arm moved away and touched the screen and the room around them shut down soon after. He lifted her in his arms and carried her out of the small white space, the panel sliding shut behind them. They headed for the central table but instead of being set down, Jack cradled her in his lap and held her. Their breathing synchronized and she felt herself relax.

"You're going to need to eat and drink more liquids. The scan indicates that you're still deficient in many nutrients and minerals. I'm sorry I did not warn you about the pricks, but now you're vaccinated for many of the common viruses found in space." She felt goosebumps over her scalp as his fingers tugged on her hair. "Your ankle is healing but at a slower than a normal rate, which is to be expected, under the circumstances. I'll be able to remove your sutures in several more days, possibly sooner if we continue to massage the medicinal salve over them." He breathed, "There are more readings if you would like to know more," trailing off.

"What else did it say?"

"Your body is going through withdrawal from something on this planet, a food source perhaps. I believe it may be the wurms." Jack narrowed his eyes. "There is a strange, missing abnormality within you."

Abnormality? My curse... Allie knew she felt sick when she didn't eat them on a regular basis but she had been so distracted she hadn't noticed the usual twitch. She couldn't imagine what it would be like to go through the effects with Jack present. Her cheeks burned hot with embarrassment. "It's the wurms."

"You have started going through the process but with the incredible amount of blood loss, the overuse of the medicinal salve and all the rest of the random shit that has happened, it may have had a chemical effect on you."

"I have some in my cave and my pouch if you haven't discarded it at some point. I'll eat one tomorrow."

"What the fuck, Allie? Of course, you're not eating that shit again, being dependent on something is not healthy." He raised his voice.

"I need to eat them. They're my main source of food here besides the roots." She raised her voice to match his.

"You'll go through withdrawal. You're never eating that shit again."

"You can't decide what I do and don't do. We're not beholden to each other and we're not friends, we made that clear." She pushed away from him but his grip tightened on her.

He stopped her struggles and cupped her chin, lifting her head to look up at him, slamming his mouth against hers. The kiss was desperate and rough.

When he had ravaged her mouth completely and all of her struggles had stopped, he whispered over her lips, "I always get what I want. I always fucking get what I want. And I think we are beholden to each other. You're never eating a goddamned bug again because you see, sweetheart, I'm taking you off this Hell-in-Space, whether you like it or not." He picked her up roughly and carried her into a passageway, past the storage unit and down a corridor she had not explored before. They entered a room that looked much like the captain's quarters and she was placed on a bed.

He tore her blanket off and threw it through the door.

Allie curled up onto the soft material beneath her, anxious from the violent look in his eyes. "What are you doing?"

"What does it look like I'm doing?" He grabbed her wrists and tied them together with a strap he unbuckled from his body armor. When she didn't answer, he answered for her. "I'm going to fuck that little hole of yours, the one that has been wet and screaming for my dick for the past week." He stared at her core, where she held her thighs tightly together, feeling the wet heat he was talking about. Her wrists were held tight in one of his hands outstretched between them.

She watched as he ran his other hand through his dark hair to rest at the back of his neck.

"Jack," she whispered.

"I've been wanting to fuck you since I crash landed here over a week ago. I smelled your cunt on that first fucking day. You can't get enough of it." His voice was hoarse and she could see his hard-on tent his armor. He snickered at her when he noticed what she was staring at. "You naughty girl, staring at my crotch. You're so far gone from what I'm saying I can taste you in the air."

He leaned forward slowly, menacingly, and placed a chaste kiss on her pouted lips. "Tell me you want it," Jack breathed softly over her mouth.

Allie swallowed her words, acutely aware that her face was flushed red; she curled her toes in anticipation. "I want – I want you. I want everything, everything you're willing to give me." Allie felt the confession come from her pounding heart.

Jack pulled away from her but didn't move far. Before she could process her thoughts, his hand had let go of hers and traveled to her thighs, pulling them apart. "Tell me to stop," he groaned. "You're broken, tell me to stop." He demanded. He had had his demands met at every turn, this time she wasn't going to give him what he thought he wanted.

Instead, she lay back slowly, opening herself up, laying her hands loosely above her head.

• • • •

JACK WAS THE ONE GOING crazy. He was between her long lithe legs with her body begging and stretched out on his bed before him. *I need to stop, turn my humanity off, walk away.* But he couldn't, he was a selfish man.

He knew he should let her heal, body and mind. Let her rest, eat, and recover. But he *was* a selfish man and right now he wanted reassurance that she was alive more than anything else in the universe.

With a full view of her pussy, he watched as she contracted her muscles – opening – trembling and wet. She was becoming uncomfortable with the vulnerability of her position, her breaths increasing with each second but he couldn't look away. She swayed her hips to prompt him but instead, he found himself enraptured by her movements when her wetness was spread all over.

"Jack," she whimpered, pushing her butt up in the air, urging him to move. He placed a hand on her hip to stop her.

"I'm enjoying the view." Her face blushed an even deeper rosy pink. "If you knew all the things I want to do to you, you would run, you would keep me from you," he confessed, picturing his cock sliding into her.

She moaned, the sound weak yet encouraging. *She is encouraging me, how can I deny her?* She was so willing.

"I don't want you to stop," she moaned, subtly pushing her hips toward him again. "If you knew all the things I wanted you to do to me, you wouldn't be hesitating." Her eyes closed. "I want you."

Her words burned him, shot through him like a spray of bullets. His reaction much the same in both situations. Violence, passion, retaliation. He dropped onto his knees between her legs on the bed and roughly penetrated her with his index finger, watching it get lost in her, any remaining tension of anticipation melted away.

"Do you feel that, sweetheart?" He pressed hard into her, flexing it, plying her sheath to open up. His finger preparing her tight cunt for his straining cock.

Jack heard her whimper yes.

She was so willing and receptive, it made it difficult to stop himself from succumbing to his baser instincts. He ensured his dick remained buckled in his pants to stop himself from doing anything rash.

Her brow glistened with perspiration as he pumped his finger into her core, flexing his thumb to rub her clit. His hand was coated in her dripping essence.

"Do you like my hand, Allie?" he groaned.

"Yes," she gasped, her hands coming forward to hold onto the arm that was currently fucking her pussy, increasing the pressure between them.

"It really likes you." He released her suddenly, pushing his finger between her soft lips. "Taste yourself." He demanded, grinding his teeth together as she hummed, her tongue swirling around it, licking it. Her pretty lips puckering around him.

"Good girl." He drew his finger out with a pop.

He leaned over her, covering her body with his and kissed her deeply, pushing his demands onto her pliant body but ever careful to not hurt her, pressing his hips between her legs until his cock was grinding heavily over her pussy. He wanted to have her scent on his pants again, rubbing along her as they warred with their mouths.

Jack liked that she had a tendency to bite his scarred lower lip. His breath hissed when her hands ran down his armored body and reached for his cock, nearly losing himself in the process, lifting up to watch her struggle to remove his pants. He smirked at her efforts.

"It's nice to know you want it as much as it wants you."

"Jack, please stop talking and help me."

He burst out in laughter, nuzzling his face into her hair, overcome with the scent of desperation all the while he could feel her pull at his crotch.

With a groan, his laughter died away, he reached down between them and unbuckled his pants. Her hand eagerly slipped between him and the material until she found his shaft. Warm fingers wrapped around his length and tugged it free. Allie's breath hitched as he sprang free, seeing him unhindered, his hard-on haloed by the dim white lights of his ship.

He was full of himself, and he knew what she was thinking at that moment as her hand cupped his girth. That he was ramrod straight, that he was as hard as hell was hot, and that it was pointed right at her. His genetics had made him perfectly endowed.

His shaft was pushed upward as his pants and buckles rested around his hips, tight over his sack. Liking the pressure it caused he left it there, instead of pushing his hips forward to glide his length between her legs. Her hand moved with him, the grip erratic as it splayed around his length, innocently exploring as it went from soft caresses to abrupt tugs. Her velvety skin moved over his beaded head, peeked with precum, and down its base.

Jack allowed her to explore him while he settled his fore-arms on either side of her head and captured her supple mouth. His fingers tangled themselves in her hair and tugged it with need.

She was weak and willing beneath him as he continued to run his hard-on over her, feeling his length get slick with her arousal.

The body lying under him opened up, becoming a beautiful vessel for his pleasure but also his own personal *Hell.*

Lust clouded his brain as she tilted her head to the side and broke their kiss. Allie's breaths deepened as her chest pulsated from each heavy lungful, her breasts pressed into his chest with each gasp. He moved his mouth down her chin, over her beating pulse, briefly latching onto her protruding collarbone to give it a light bite. He felt her body twitch from the strange sensation.

"Tell me to stop," he whispered, licking his way down to her perky nipples.

Instead of responding, she moved her locked hands and tangled them in his unruly hair, urging him on. His cock was sad to lose the heated grip of her hands.

"Your tits remind me of raspberries," he moaned right before he latched onto one and sucked it into his mouth. His thumb and forefinger caught the other one and rolled the hard peak.

"I've never had raspberries," she moaned.

Jack looked up at her face as he ran his tongue along the underside of her breasts, his hands on both sides cupping them together, squeezing them. He watched as every time he pinched one of her hard nipples, her teeth would bite down on her bottom lip; it was driving him crazy.

He reared up on his knees to look down at her flushed body, taking in every inch of her form until she opened her eyes and met his gaze.

The world around him shattered when she gave him a soft, sated smile.

"Jack," she continued to smile up at him, killing him. "I would do anything for you."

He narrowed his eyes at her confession as an unusual feeling pulsated through his system and it made him want to shudder as if he could shake it off. Possession strangled his heart.

Below him her core burned, the muscles quivered, making the soft lips of her pussy pulsate. He lifted her legs up and settled them around his waist and he pushed the head of his cock into her, his precum spread over her tight entrance. Mindless with wanton desire, he watched her little hole take him in, squeezing the life out of it as it demanded submission.

He looked up at her face before he took her completely. "We're both idiots," he whispered as he thrust the rest of the way into her.

Her body arched off the bed in a breathless gasp, her face scrunched in pleasure and then winced in pain. Jack could read her body easily in such close proximity; he had been unconsciously transferring his cybercells over her and knew it was her bruised ankle that was the cause. He rounded his hand under her knee and held her leg out from their joined bodies as he slowly, deliberately thrust into her, preventing it from moving with his steely grip. Her discomfort quickly eased and the tensed muscles of her restrained leg went lax.

He pushed into her with every whimper, fueled by her body's sinuous writhing.

"I need to know you're alive," he ground out, his eyes narrowed on where they were joined as he pulled out and vigorously thrust back in. With his free hand, he rubbed her glistening clit, desperate to feel her body climax under and around him.

"Please," she cried, her hands clawed at his chest, grasping his armor.

"I need to feel you, sweetheart." He tweaked her nub. His fingers pushed her lips apart while his middle continued to rub her, needing to watch her stretched tight around his shaft. The connection meant everything to him at that moment.

He drove into her several more times before she tensed up around him, her legs moving wildly as she pulled herself upward. Her grip strengthened on his weapon's straps, riding the waves of her orgasm over him.

When her body stopped quivering and her hold loosened up, Jack gently pushed her back down into the bed, keeping his hold steady on her leg. He fucked her fast and hard as he leaned over her breasts and bit down on a bouncing nipple, climaxing in her yielding cunt a moment later.

Jack pushed up and kissed her swollen, bitten lips. Her eyes were closed and her breaths heavy from their frantic lovemaking. He buried his tongue into her mouth while he continued to pump into her, unable to break their link.

It wasn't until he began to feel her body loosen up with sleep that he unmounted her, careful of her leg and the worst of her bruises. He tumbled onto his back and pulled her sleeping form close.

Chapter Fifteen:

• • • •

There was something beneath her that was soft and warm, and it felt alien to her. Her body was cushioned from head to toe on every side as if she was suspended inside a fluffy cloud.

She snuggled deeper into the soft warmth, pulling her legs up and twisting her arms into silky, cool blankets as her naked body took in every square inch of comfort. She could smell Jack in the cloth: a mixture of metal and man, with a hint of the crisp sterilization of the ship. If she had a choice, she would never move again.

If I could wake up in clouds every morning, my life would be a good one.

Allie knew she could not stay though and forced her weak, aching muscles to wake up, quickly realizing that Jack was not lying next to her. She became consumed with thoughts of the frenetic joining the night before, wanting him all over again. Now she was alone.

Her eyes snapped open. *He's going to take me off of this planet.*

She sat up, her free hands rubbing over her wrists, the straps he had tied around them gone. The panel door was wide open across the room, alleviating her abrupt fear that he might keep her with him against her will.

If she was going to contemplate escape, it would be extremely difficult with a man like Jack. He seemed to know everything. *He probably knows I'm awake.* His confession alone that he knew she had been watching him when he had first arrived was proof enough. She hadn't known what he was then, and even if she had, she still would have watched him; however, she might not have entered his ship.

Why am I not frightened?

Did she want to leave this planet? *Yes.* Was she comfortable assimilating to a new world? *Depends.* Did she want to be alone? *No.*

It was settled. A weight lifted off of her shoulders because she would stay with him and she would leave with him. *Maybe he'll let me choose where I'll end up.*

Allie looked around the cabin. It was simply decorated, with dim lights that wrapped around the exterior walls, and a similar circular light ring on the ceiling like several of the other rooms on the ship. The bed she was sitting on was connected to the wall like the one in the medical bay and there was a large transparent screen that blipped numbers and letters directly across from her. Above the exterior light ring was a large line of shiny chrome shutters that were tightly closed. She wondered if they opened up to a viewing glass.

I wonder what it would be like to lie on this cloud-like bed and stare out at the stars?

At the end of the shutters there was a closed panel door down a short flight of steps and on the last wall, where the open door was located, stood a white metal shelf divided into large squares; each of the squares housed a strange assortment of items.

On one shelf there was a blackened glass screen with a keypad, another had a shallow crystal bowl that was brimming with silvery liquid, and the third shelf had a stack of old, peeling books. There were weapons, stones, and other items that she could not place. *Jack must be a collector.* These things must have some value to him if he kept them in his room, or at least she assumed it was his room.

Allie wrapped the blanket around her and slowly stood up, testing the strength of her feet. The swelling on her ankle had gone down significantly, but blue bruises still splotched her skin. She could walk as long as she did not put the majority of her weight on it. A dull pain settled in her joints.

She limped around the bed and used the wall as a support as she moved toward the closed panel, hoping it was a lavatory of some kind. The door slid open as she descended the three steps toward it.

Peeking inside, she saw a washroom unlike the ones she had used in her previous life. The room was stark white with light grey undertones. The light gave it a clinical look and made the room glow in its brightness. A large shower stall took up the second half of the room and a small flat sink stuck out of the white metal paneling; opposite the sink was a large cabinet that ran from floor to ceiling. Curious, Allie shuffled over to it and opened it up.

Inside was long streams of gleaming wiring, a myriad of circuit boards in different shapes and sizes, robotic parts, and other electronic pieces secured about. There was even an entire cybernetic arm; its metal fingers hung limp at the end. *These must be replacement parts for Jack.*

The humanoid machinery temporarily stunned her. She was used to seeing Jack the man, but now that she had a glimpse of the hidden cyber-robotic parts, it confused her. *Jack is unlike me, why do I keep forgetting that? He's part machine, of course, he would have extra parts stored in his living quarters.* Allie shook her head, feeling the cobwebs come back.

Was he more human or was he more machine? And maybe it was a good thing that he wasn't entirely human. Humans tended to suffer around her. A Cyborg may be able to survive her bad karma, the curse that clung to her existence.

"Looking for something?"

Allie jumped at the sound of his voice and turned to face him, her hold on the blanket draped around her tightening. "Someplace to clean myself." She gaped at him. Jack was shirtless and leaning against the door frame, his muscles straining with his arms crossed over his chest. His hair clung to him like he had just washed, but the smudges of dirt and sand that plastered his boots said otherwise.

Jack straightened up and stalked toward her, reaching around her to close the cabinet door. A light hum filled the space as a screen appeared on the wall next to them. He punched a series of numbers in and the washroom changed. A large showerhead manifested from the corner of the stall and gushed water out like a miniature crystalline waterfall.

The gleam of the white metal and bright lights created sparkles in the liquid, and the droplets that landed on the floor resembled diamonds. The cascade of water pooled over the tile, leveling out at their feet and then sucked into hidden vents around the edges.

A relief basin appeared next to the small sink as the cabinet sunk into the wall and was replaced with a long mirror.

"Is that better?" He stepped away from the screen and watched her.

"It's incredible. Yes, thank you." Allie spun in a circle, "I didn't know technology could do things like this–" she mused until she spied a brick of soap that appeared on a shelf in the large water stall. "Soap!" She scuttled closer to it and almost tripped on the blanket that was now water-logged at the bottom edges. A warm steel hand wrapped around her upper arm.

"Careful," he snapped, righting her.

"Do you mind if I use the facilities?" She looked at him, his closeness firing up her desire. The mere presence of him caused her stomach to clench but her mind was distracted, solely focused on the fresh bar of soap that was within reach.

"You're asking now?" He grinned, letting her go and stepping back.

"Yes?" She almost felt sorry as she reached over to the stiff pink bar and cradled it between her hands, lifting the treasure to her nose. Her body contracted when she took a deep breath, her nose filled with the foreign scent. She smelled flowers. *Flowers.* The burn of tears formed in her eyes. *I haven't smelled something so beautiful or fresh in so long.*

"What smell is this?" she whispered.

"Raspberry." He smirked.

"It smells like flowers." She sniffed the bar again.

He laughed. "No. It's a berry native to Earth. You remind me of them, it suits my obsession." She was reminded of his comments about her nipples, blushing. "I'll make sure we find you some to try," he jested.

"I would like that." She finished, not knowing what to do next. Awkwardly, she held the bar to her nose and watched him across the small space that was now filling up with steam. Jack was once again propped up at the doorway, unmoving. "Are you going to leave?" she hedged.

"I'm thinking about it."

Allie's heart skipped a beat. She wanted him to stay. Her skin prickled with heat as the dew of the humid mist settled over her. Her loose, tangled hair curled up over and around her shoulders as tendrils plastered her shoulders and cheeks.

Turning away from his domineeringly relaxed form, she stepped under the cascading water, dropping the blanket on the floor before she lost her confidence.

The overflowing water drenched her in moments. It pooled and flowed around her tense form, enveloping her like a lover's embrace. Allie was part of the waterfall now and the sensation of the warm water rolling over her was heavenly. She hadn't bathed like this since the night she had been chosen by the Warlord in preparation of the primitive mating ritual.

It made sense.

She ran her fingers through her knotted hair, collecting it at her back, and turned around to face him. He was watching her like a predator about to make a kill, and he had moved closer. His hands were yanking at the buckles that strapped his belted black pants.

Waiting for him, she ran the bar of raspberry soap over her body, the fragrance igniting in the air from the glistening heat.

The next moment she was pressed into the stall wall with his hand running over her delicate curves. They rounded her thighs and lifted her up until she was propped up on his hips. Without warning, he impaled her onto his shaft.

She clawed at his shoulders as his hands cupped her butt, pounding into her, pushing her flush into the wall. All she could do was hold on as he used her; she could hear herself mew each time he pulled out and thrust back into her. The sensation of being filled then losing him every other second was driving her up the wall – *literally*. Allie entwined her fingers into his wet hair and dug her nails into his scalp.

"Jack," she pleaded. "I can't."

The pressure on the wall lessened as he bent down and licked her neck and at the same time he reached forward between them and rubbed her clit, causing her body to rupture with a scream. Her core clenched down around his straining cock.

Jack pushed her back into the wall with a groan and pummeled her until he climaxed; for once it seemed he was exerting enough energy to lose his breath. It filled her with a sensual power – that she could break his control. A hot liquid spread inside her and dripped down her legs.

He set her down a short time later and picked up the bar of soap she had dropped. The water fell over him and pushed his damp hair over his face, the dark locks caressed his scars. An uneasy, giddy feeling filled her stomach at the sight and she wanted him all over again.

"I know what you're thinking." He gave her one of his sexy grins.

"You do?" She used his shoulder as a support as he ran the soap over her legs.

"You like me." He slipped the sudsy bar between her legs, lathering up her pussy. Her feminine parts deliciously ached with his ministrations and continued to pulsate from her recent orgasm as he cleaned her.

She stared at the top of his head, unsure how to answer. "Do you like me?" His finger slid into her.

"I like you a lot," he said as he leaned forward and kissed her nub. He pulled his soapy finger out of her and guided it through her slick lips, ending at her back. She jerked away from him but he held her firm. "Tell me you like me." He licked her clit while the rough pad of his finger circled her back entrance.

"I like you," she squeaked, her legs melted as his hot tongue rolled her nub.

"Tell me you want me."

"I–I want you." Her nails dug into his shoulders as he forced her to the edge. His thumb now pushing into her ass.

"Tell me you'll stay with me." He stopped and looked up at her.

"I'll stay with you," she whispered.

"Allie," he groaned as he sucked on her clit and pressed further in. Her body collapsed from the onslaught as another orgasm ripped through. He caught her exhausted body in his arms and held her tightly as she burrowed into his chest, the water cleansing both of them. Allie couldn't imagine being anywhere else in the cosmos other than in his arms.

• • • •

JACK HELPED HER WASH after claiming her in the shower. He had lost his mind when she brazenly dropped her sheath and stepped under the sparkling water, goading him into joining her.

She was everything he needed, everything he wanted. He looked at her and envisioned courage, pain, and fortitude. He saw an innocent hope. Allie wasn't pretentious, never expected anything from him, and didn't shy away from his Cyborg nature. She was the embodiment of wild – of what he felt so deeply within himself. *I need wild hope.*

I need her sincerity.

He would never have to hold himself back with her because deep down inside he knew she was just as imperfect as he was. They were blank slates that were just waiting to be filled with each other and Jack wanted her slate to be filled up with nothing but himself.

Blank slates, my ass, more like rusted steel plates that need a good scrubbing.

Jack helped her dress in new soft cotton clothing he had the replicator create while she was asleep a loose, sleeveless tunic and tight formfitting leggings.

"Do I have to wear these?" She pulled at the clothing cinching her ankles. He laughed at her pained look.

"No." He pulled her pants off in one quick tug. She had reacted as he had expected until he watched in dismay as she took the pants from him, grabbed a dagger off the table and cut them in half; shuffling back into them. Now they only reached her knees.

"What's wrong?" she asked, picking up the extra cloth.

He took the dagger from her hand. "Nothing." Disappointment laced his voice. "I need to do a couple of final repairs on the impulse drive before we can leave." He held out his arm for her to lean on. "I've been working while you were sleeping. The circuitry I salvaged is installed and functioning but will need to be replaced as soon as possible."

Jack led her outside to the damaged side of his ship. The jagged scar that streaked over the outside away from his impulse drives stood out in the midday light. He frowned, wishing he had Pirate Captain Larik's throat in his hands. *When my ship is damaged, I'm damaged.*

"That was what made your ship crash? The impulse drive?"

"It got hit by several meteors while I was in pursuit of my target. The second hit knocked the plating to the circuitries. The stress of the landing and impact on the surface burned them out." He let go of her to run his hand over his ship, transferring more of his nanobots for good measure.

"What's that?" He heard her choke on her words. She was pointing at the black plating, the ones he had taken from the crash site and used to replace the gaping parts to his ship's exterior.

"It's the metal we took. The ones we picked up outside the reactor," he said slowly, watching her. The black plating stuck out like a sore thumb against the silvery blue gleam of the rest of his flyer.

"It's cursed, Jack." Allie took a step back as she continued to stare at it unblinkingly.

"It's metal."

"It's *cursed* metal."

"How do you figure?" He sighed.

"Because everything from that ship is cursed. I'm cursed." She exhaled. "I didn't think of it when you picked up the stuff but now that I see it, I see everything that's attached to it, and to me." She hugged herself. "It's still with me. I can feel it eroding my mind, pulling me into the darkness. I don't like it."

"Allie," he clutched her hand. "It's just metal. We can't leave this planet safely without it, and I'm not leaving this planet without you."

"Are you so sure? It could curse you too. It will coax your thoughts and swallow you whole at night. It will whisper in your head and those whispers won't be yours. You'll live with the heaviness of something watching you, waiting for you, manipulating you every day." Her voice had gone emotionless and numb.

Jack was unnerved by her words. Why was he just hearing this now? Why hadn't she told him more before they had gone to the crash site? "Is that what happens with you? Why that shipwreck had felt wrong? It was cursed. You were a part of it and now you think you're cursed too? How do you explain how you survived then? *Twice*?" He placed his hands over the black metal, forcing the bots he had transferred earlier into the foreign pieces to scan it.

"Ophelia saved me. You saved me the second time but she wasn't there anymore. I need to know where she is."

"Your friend," he stated, his bots moving through the black metal, coming up with nothing odd.

"Yes."

"Do you think this all ties to her?" he asked, flinching as his nanobots died, deteriorating at a rapid rate inside the plating. He didn't try to save them.

"She used to talk to the darkness," was her only answer.

"Where do you think she is, if not here?" He stepped back to stand next to Allie, staring with her at the black blemish on his once pristine ship.

"I don't know." Her voice sounded crestfallen as he gathered her in his arms and held her tight, running his lips over the top of her head, the still-wet strands dampening his skin.

"At the first opportunity, I'll dispose of the metal," he promised. "Allie, you're not cursed, and even if you were–are, I would do everything in my power to destroy it. I wish you had told me all of this before I asked you to take me to that place."

"You would never have believed me." She was right and he didn't believe her now about being cursed, only that the things that had inhabited that ship were otherworldly and he would have kept her away from it.

Instead of agreeing with her he cupped her cheeks and lifted her head to face him. "I saw that thing in the cave, the same one you killed. I believe *that*. I heard wailing shrieks when I went to look for you in the ruined passages and I believe that too. All of it warns of the irrationality of it all, but I can't deny my experiences." He expected tears to drip down her face from the exhaustive trauma but her eyes remained wide and dry.

"If I'm not cursed, then I don't know what to do." Her eyes fluttered closed.

"You heal. It will be hard, and each day will be different. Some battles don't end at the edge of a dagger or a bullet through the heart but are fought every single day in your mind." He kissed the tip of her nose. "I will help you." She leaned forward into him and he cocooned her within his arms, clasping her to his chest. Her body shook as the tears came forward. He held her close as she collapsed against him sobbing.

Chapter Sixteen:

· · · ·

I t was approaching nightfall when he sensed a shift in the air, like a small annoying breeze that tickled a single strand of hair. It probed his senses subtly and then would go away just to return again a moment later. It was getting worse.

He had set Allie up on a communications device to read about anything she desired; anything to get her mind off of her troubled thoughts.

They had encountered a small hitch in the setup because of her language barrier. Hers was a dialect crossed between Earthian and a primitive form of Trentian. It would be enough to get her by in most space sectors, especially with him by her side, but she would have to learn more. At least enough of one language to hold a detailed conversation with a stranger. Jack reconfigured his systems to verbally queue upon request and switched its base language to Trentian which is what she could read.

He had been monitoring the process of his ship as it healed itself. The systems were just about recalibrated with the new, worn parts that were installed. They would be leaving this Hell-in-Space tonight—together.

A tingle rolled over the back of his neck.

He rubbed it absently as he routed electrical channels back to the foreign paneling, rescanning it for the dozenth time that day. Once again he came away with nothing. *It's just metal,* he kept telling himself as there were no unusual properties to be found, that it was only worn tungsten that had seen better days.

Why was it agitating him? After the last week, he wasn't about to dismiss any possibility, there was already too much he couldn't explain and the last thing he wanted was to bring the crap of this planet off with them.

At the first opportunity, he would ditch the parts and be rid of the junk, especially if it made Allie happy. It was just a matter of time now.

"Jack, I think you should come look at this." He swiveled in his chair, Allie was standing by the view glass looking outside. He could see unusual movement beyond her.

He jumped up and went to her side and surveyed the landscape. The usually still terrain was now being pummeled with gusts of wind; dirt and sand were being pulled up from the ground in a violent swirl. It was thickening by the second.

"It's a sandstorm," she whispered. A loud thunderous boom rang through his ears as a wall of sand clouds towered high and formed in the distance; monstrous static bolts crashed and crackled amidst the gusts. He clenched his hand; any moment they were going to lose visual.

There was no more time to wait. *We need to take off now.*

"Say goodbye to Hell, Allie." He lifted her up and settled her into the co-pilot's seat, strapping her in. "Prepare for take-off, it's going to be a blast." He would have snickered if the situation was less dire.

Jack clambered into the captain's chair and strapped in. There was nothing but golden brown sand swiping across his view screen and it was darkening by the second.

Placing his hands on his ship's activation pads, he connected with his engines for the first time in nearly two weeks, powering them on. He forced the last of the diagnostics in record time as he initiated lift off.

A powerful vibration surged throughout the metal frame as every wire, circuit, and processor flooded with electrical energy. The power flowed through his ship, back through him, and then back through his ship again; he felt at home at last.

Now Allie would be a part of it too. He would teach her how to copilot, and install some big energy cannons she could control. *She may want her own cybernetic enhancements in the future.* His thoughts briefly drifted as he mulled over the possibility.

"Jack, are you sure—"

"It's too late now, the wurms are enraged. We take off now or we die." He cut her off. He pushed his impulse drives, deluging them with energy; the newly repaired one was taking longer to charge than normal. The lights flickered as a loud impact hit the top of his ship and they lifted off of the ground.

"What the fuck? If there is one more scratch on my ship I'm going to blow up this planet."

"Jack, go up!" Allie screamed. Static lightning hit the ground before them, illuminating the landscape in flashes. The biggest wurm he had ever seen shot out from the ground. If it landed on them, they would be crushed.

Allie's knuckles went white beside him, clutching the armrests of the chair. *She's going to crush them.* Her mouth was hanging open in a silent scream.

"Sweetheart, I should be the only one making you scream." He teased as he thrust his ship skyward and propelled forward, narrowly missing a legion of giant wurm heads bursting from the ground. His ship jerked from the stress, momentarily faltering as his systems caught up. He could feel microchemical reactions, catalysts initiating, and electrical explosions throughout his ship's reactor as it struggled to supply enough charge throughout the vessel. It made him giddy with adrenaline.

Jack kept his eyes on the storm before him but his mind was with his ship. He used his cybernetics to right any wrong with his systems, ensuring no major malfunctions would occur, that nothing would overheat during acceleration. If he could pilot a flagship battlecruiser during the war, he could handle anything his personal battle flyer could throw at him.

They slowly but steadily ascended into the sandy sky, at times dodging as large rocks flew by and blasts of static lightning struck. It was only when they were clear of the forest of wurms that violent winds tore at his vessel. The winds acted like giant hands, pushing them off course, demanding that they come back to the destructive surface.

He put everything he had in that moment to break through the ghostly barrier.

A tortured wail erupted around them as his ship broke through the sandy wall, moving above the riotous winds.

Allie was as white as a wraith, struggling with her straps and vomiting over the side of the chair.

Below them, a giant series of derecho storms spotted Argo's surface, centralizing where their ship had been located. Even *he* could see the violent blasts of golden lightning litter the storm clouds from his vantage point. They looked like long skeletal fingers scratching at the planet.

Red lights blared around them just as they broke into the thermosphere. His ship canted as it flew toward the stars.

"What's happening now?" she squeaked.

Jack steadied his ship and opened up the intercom screen, reconnecting with the intergalactic network. The screens covered up a wide berth of his view station as information downloaded into his ship's database. The atmospheric barrier of the planet must have stopped any signal from coming through.

"It's a distress beacon." His smile transformed into a wide, evil grin. *I'm taking cues from a shadow demon.* "It's the man I have been hunting." He felt his luck changing the further they flew away from Argo.

"Your mission?"

"I'm a bounty hunter, Allie, and it looks like I'm about to catch my prey." He maneuvered his flyer to follow the beacon, inputting the coordinates as another giddy rush of energy coursed through his body.

• • • •

ALLIE HAD BEEN SCARED before, terrified on several occasions, some of those occasions happened to be very recent. But the nauseous gut reaction, the speed of change, and having a front row seat made her want to curl up in a corner and die. Everything was happening right before her eyes as the co-pilot's seat had an 180-degree view.

One moment she had been reading up on the communications system, standing up to look at the window, and the next they were initiating emergency lift-off procedures. She had been reading up on cybernetics when an unusual movement caught her eye. She had turned to look, moving closer to the reinforced glass window when a splatter of dirt blew past the gloss. Speckles of dust stuck to the panes upon impact.

Peering out over the landscape, gusts of sand were flying in erratic patterns for miles in every direction. It was the beginning of a sandstorm and it was developing fast, faster than she had ever seen before. Allie felt the color drain from her face. Her muscles twitched in anticipation, urging her to run for cover.

The color had yet to return and she still wanted to run screaming but there was no place to run. They were flying above the storm now and she couldn't see the surface of the planet anymore while with every heartbeat the ship picked up speed and moved further away from her former life. She watched as what had been her life and her home for the past half-decade fell away, becoming an insignificant orb amongst the stars.

She had never thought she would leave 'HIS', that she would exist on its surface until death came for her. Her entire world was changing so quickly that it was hard to make sense of it.

The planet was now a golden speck in the distance as Jack's ship flew further into the void.

Allie took several deep breaths to calm her nerves. Each frayed ending had been on the brink of explosion for so long that she couldn't recall what it felt like to be relaxed.

"It's our lucky night."

She turned toward Jack with a modicum of apprehension, wary of what he meant by 'lucky'. *At least I'm saying goodbye to the planet and not to him.* "Because we survived?" Allie couldn't keep the cynicism out of her voice. Every day she spent in his presence the more her outlook on life changed.

"We'll always survive." He grumbled at her. "That distress signal," he flourished his hand toward the blinking red lights before them, "is from Captain Larik's ship. It's moving at a slow speed. He's either adrift in space or attached to an asteroid." Jack laughed, the sound evil with just a hint of glee.

"He's the man you're hunting?"

"Yes. He's the piece of shit that led me all the way here to the fringes of Trentian air space."

Confused, she asked, "Why are you hunting him? Did he hurt you?" She was curious about his motivations.

"I've taken a contract and my current employers, the Earthian Council, require his capture–for a myriad of crimes. Once I capture my target, I'll receive a bounty. Hence, bounty hunter." She jerked back in her seat as he sent his ship into warp drive. The next moment a cluster of giant rocks expanded before them, floating aimlessly through space. "You're now my partner." He looked over and grinned at her.

"What do you mean, 'your partner?' I don't know how to bounty hunt." Allie's eyes widened as he moved forward to float between the asteroids, keeping the ship just far enough away to not collide.

"You'll learn. Tonight," he stated with stern authority, brokering an end to the subject.

Allie just couldn't get a break. *If I could still see my Hell-in-Space I would probably look at it longingly.* Her stomach swelled up in disgust at the thought.

Jack got up from his seat and came over to her, unbuckling her straps and helped her stand. "How are you feeling?" His eyes flashed. He was reading her.

"I feel everything," she murmured honestly.

His enchanting smirk lit up his intense face as his eyes bore into her and penetrated her soul; he was cyborging on her again. "That's good. It means you're alive." He offered his arm. "Come with me. It's time to suit up."

A little while later they were in the double thick, locked room off of the storage unit and Jack was fully dressed in his battle armor, guns, daggers, and clips that were strapped to his body with thick black military-grade buckles. He frightened her when he exuded an almost overkilll aura of lethality.

But the room made her feel oddly secure. She had stumbled after seeing what was stored within.

Guns.

Hundreds of them, all different. There were guns displayed on every wall around her, some as small as her hand while others were as large as her body. Cases of ammo sat behind concealed laser barriers. Scattered throughout the dull grey mass of weaponry were long knives, daggers, swords, and sets of armor. It had to be the biggest room on the ship except for the central room and the cockpit.

What was she going to do with this stuff? She didn't know how to use a gun.

Instead, she decided to stand back quietly and observe Jack suiting up. She watched as he picked out choice weapons from the walls and equipped them; one gun in particular clipped over his arm like it was being plugged in. It powered to life and sent an electric blue streak up to his neck. The light still haloed him although the gun appeared to immediately power off.

"Why does your armor have blue streaks of light?" She was curious.

Jack stopped what he was doing and looked at his arm. He ran his finger over the source. "It's specially made Cyborg armor. It connects into our cybernetics." He turned around to continue gearing up. "It glows for one reason only," he paused for a moment. "So our enemies would be attracted to us as targets and not to the fragile humans around us."

"Why do you still wear it then?"

"Because it works. It works very well," he said ominously.

Once he had buckled the last strap, she had to will herself to step forward because he looked like he did that first day: a dangerous enigma of a man, exuding the lethality and power that was needed to own everything he laid his eyes on.

She had been lured in herself but it wasn't because of the weapons or the clothes he wore. It was because of the man underneath.

Allie wanted to tear off his bodysuit and find that warm-blooded man underneath. She wanted her Cyborg bounty hunter all to herself. Why did he have to leave to capture this man now that they had the freedom to explore the stars?

Feeling a little crazy, moderately emboldened, and frustrated beyond belief, she plucked a conservatively sized gun off the wall and pointed it at him.

He looked at her, his eyes slowly moving up and down her body as a devilish smirk twisted his lips. "Good choice, not my first pick for you but you've always exceeded my expectations." Her blood heated as a girlish blush materialized over her skin.

"What?" Confused and oddly pleased she looked at the gun in her hand.

He walked over to her and slid his thumb down the side, the handle heated up under her palm. "This is a semi-automatic laser pistol." He turned it in her hand, "Point at your target and pull this trigger." He showed her a curved black nob. "There will be a little recoil but it won't hurt you." He continued, reaching around her and pulling a heavy vest over her head – which appeared like magic – strapping the uncomfortable padding down her sides. "Don't get trigger happy, laser pistols don't have clips like normal pistols do but they will overheat and burn out. Make your shots count."

"Jack, I don't think I can do this," she said, feeling the strange alien weight around her.

"Of course you can. It's the best therapy for people like us." He curled a tendril of her hair around his finger. "Allie, you won't have to do anything but pretend. Point the gun at our target, Larik. If he moves toward you or tries to get away, if he aims a gun or brandishes a knife, shoot. But it won't come to that." He stepped back and looked at her. "All you need now are some sturdy combat boots, my cute little bounty hunter."

Jack picked up a spare pair of boots from one of the armor sets and threw them into a box on the wall, punching in a code. When a light flashed he opened the box and pulled the shoes back out. "Put these on."

With an exasperated sigh, she stuck her feet into the tough material. The boots were padded but it did nothing to alleviate her swollen foot. *It's better than going barefoot.* She looked down at the warm gun in her hand and wondered how she had ended up here.

A light tug on her hair brought her back to the present as Jack came up behind her and pulled her tangled waves back, tying them loosely at the base of her neck. "You never want anything on or near your head that might block your sight when in the field." He tugged her hair and turned her around, perusing her from head to toe. "I can't wait to tear all of this off of you later."

Allie's fingers twitched in arousal. She had been thinking the same thing about him just minutes ago. "Agreed," she breathed.

His leather encased hands cupped her face as he leaned down to kiss her. Their tongues warred in excitement and desperation. When he pulled away, she gasped deeply, filling her deprived lungs. "Do you think I'll be good at this?"

After everything that I have survived, I really don't want to die now. Not without him. Not without experiencing what a life with him would be like.

"You're going to be great. Listen to me and you can do anything, just remember–"

"Aim to kiss," she interrupted. "Err, I mean kill. Kill," Allie said, flustered.

He grinned. "Yes. Always." Jack grabbed two visors off of a shelf. "Unless we need our target alive. Any kiss you give a strange man will be a kiss of death." He placed one over her head, a clear transparent screen covered her eyes. "Take my arm, this next part is going to be bumpy."

When she latched onto him he placed his hand on a keypad on the wall, going stone-still. The ship jerked beneath her; a tug of gravity hollowed out her stomach. He took her arm and led her back to the cockpit, moving toward their designated chairs.

Jack stopped her and seized her waist, sitting her on his lap before strapping the two of them in. "You stay with me." He said as one arm coiled around her while the other reconnected with his ship. They flew through the rocky belt at a breakneck speed.

Allie wanted to be connected with him as he connected with his ship. She wanted to feel him in every molecule of her being as an urge to be a part of the circuit of his life filled her broken soul. He was warm, solid, and safe, and she was beginning to believe that nothing could happen to him, even her cursed self.

"Look." He nudged her shoulder with his chin.

Right outside the view screen, a small black ship was attached to an asteroid. They were close enough that she could see right through and into a darkened cockpit.

The vessel was like a spider clinging for life with no web to break its fall. The mechanized flyer, smaller than Jack's ship, was a bundle of metal carnage.

A quick spark pulsated over the crystalline glass barrier, briefly obstructing her view. They were gliding forward, the structure growing before her eyes. A static pop nipped her ears, followed by a steady stream of white noise as an unfamiliar voice crackled through the room. She was unable to locate its source.

"Of course you're alive."

"It's nice of you to wait for me, Pirate, you really didn't have to," Jack taunted her.

"Fuck you, Cyborg." The static barrage of the unknown male's voice grated her nerves.

A blast of black shrapnel erupted from the metal mass as cylindrical drones filled the distance between them. Jack laughed as his ship tilted dramatically to the right as huge chrome plating opened up before them on both sides and pushed forward as cannon-like structures descended into its vacated space. The giant guns dropped their safety as beautiful blue streaks, similar to Jack's armor, blazed around the openings.

The cannons aimed at each drone, assaulting them with continuous streams of bright lasers. The colors lit up the dark void of space, blasting each battle-drone until they ruptured. Dozens of bots cracked with fissures of energy just before they ceased to exist. Orange plasma fire flared out like bullets amongst the intense streams until each drone disintegrated into dust.

Jack's ship had barely moved. Not one hit made it through.

"Is that all you have, Larik? I must say, I'm disappointed." Jack sighed. "And here I thought you were a challenge."

"Cut the crap, robot, you can see my ship's cannons are damaged. I'm just fucking happy that it's lifeless enough that you can't infect it with any real effect."

"I can control a vessel that's running on generators." Jack's fingers twitched as the broken junk before them lit up.

"But you can't make it fly. Come and get me, I'm growing tired of this conversation." The static vanished with a fizzle. Allie's ears opened up with relief.

Jack was quiet as he maneuvered his ship next to the pirate's broken one. A translucent green shield tunneled out to the hatch of the other ship. A layer of silver framework slid over and joined the vessels together, creating a passageway between them.

She was out of Jack's lap now and pressed up against the abyss-cold glazed glass, enthralled by the floating debris and colors. She knew Jack was controlling everything, even the foreign ship as it met the tunnel halfway. His abilities were fascinating and frightening. *I'm happy that I'm not the one being hunted.*

Allie looked down at the gun still in her hand and wondered if he could control that too.

"There is only one life form on his ship. If he had crewmates, they are dead." He got up and exited the cockpit, motioning for her to follow. They walked down through the central hub and toward the docked passageway.

When they reached the door he turned to face her. "I want you to wait here. Keep your body behind the door, only look if you absolutely need to." He lifted her hand with the gun. "If anyone tries to get through, shoot them. Never hesitate–*they* won't."

"I–I don't know how to shoot." Her battered nerves short-circuited.

"Pretend. Be confident. They don't know what you know." He checked his weapons, all of them much larger and scarier than hers. "I'm 98.8 percent positive that you will encounter nothing. If I felt this situation was at all dangerous, you would be far, far away from it," he said as he stopped what he was doing to bore into her eyes. His were sparkling storms, the glisten from the visor enhancing his most unnerving feature. "I need to know that you're near. I need you close to me so I can protect you. You wouldn't even be here right now if this wasn't a great opportunity to start your training. I never dock my ship with my enemies under normal circumstances." He went on, trying to make her understand.

I do understand. I need you close to me too.

Jack turned away from her as the hatch opened. "I'll be back in a few minutes." He stepped through.

"I love you," she blurted quickly, stammering her words. Allie crushed her teeth against her bottom lip.

He stopped in his tracks. She let her feelings leave her and settle in the air between them to be caught or to float away.

"I love you too."

She watched as he disappeared into the weighted gloom.

Chapter Seventeen:

· · · ·

His steps were soft, but they didn't need to be. He had control of Larik's ship and he knew where his heat signature was located. The man was sitting at the helm of his broken ship, eerily still in the captain's seat.

Even if he didn't have the blueprint ingrained in his mind, Jack would have been able to locate the pirate by his breathing alone. The man was relatively relaxed, his breaths quiet and sad. *Just not quiet enough for a Cyborg to miss.*

Jack wondered why Larik was making this so easy for him.

He passed through the ship with ease, dust mites and unsterilized dirt glided behind him in his wake. He was impressed with the heavy dark appeal of it, even the interior trappings matched in style and mood. Shadows clung to the ship like a death shroud.

It was half the size of his but was decked out to the nines like a fallout bunker. The only color besides the oppressing black was a military gunmetal green. Jack would never have pictured Larik as such a stoic, combat-ready man.

He clipped his gun back into place and dimmed the streaks of light on his armor as he entered the helm. "That's it? No fight?" He clicked his visor up and perused his surroundings.

Larik was hunched over in the captain's seat, his elbows resting in defeat on his knees, staring at a revolver in his hands. "Have you come here to kill me or capture me?"

"Capture. You pissed off the wrong people this time, Larik."

The man sighed, "It was a risk worth taking."

"Mmm." Jack understood his meaning. "Was it a woman?"

Larik's weapon went limp in his hand, only held up by his finger through the trigger. "It was for an ideal."

Fuck idealists. "You're known throughout the inhabited galaxies, Captain Larik, Commander of a legion of outlaws and pirates. Organized intergalactic crime. What kind of ideal does a man like you have?" He was incredulous.

"You might find this surprising, Cyborg, but we're the good guys." He sighed. "I'm tired. Let's get this over with." He stood up and turned the handle of the revolver over to him. Jack took the ancient weapon and led Larik out.

When they approached the hatch, he stopped the pirate and called out. "Allie, we're coming through." Larik turned toward him with a look of surprise.

Jack grabbed the back of his vest and pushed him forward, shutting down the ship behind him and closing the second hatch. Allie stepped out of her hiding place behind the door and checked out the new man.

He felt an unusual flame of jealousy course through his systems, both halves equally affected by his abrupt possessiveness. It didn't help that Larik dug his feet in, bringing them to a halt in front of her.

"A girl?" he asked, nodding his head toward him.

"Keep moving, she's none of your business," he ground out.

"You'd better listen to him." Allie swung her charged gun between Larik and him, making them both jerk back. "He's a Cyborg."

"Is he now?" Larik smirked.

Jack unceremoniously pushed him forward. "Keep. Moving." He led Larik into his ship and forced him to break eye contact with Allie. He could hear her follow quietly behind them.

Once he threw Larik into the brig and sealed the entrance with a laser shield, he relaxed his tense muscles. He watched as Larik settled his back into the cushioned wall and slid down, his arms loosely draped over his knees.

"Where are you taking me?"

"Taggert."

The pirate swiped his hand over his long golden dreadlocks and swore. "That's going to be a bitch to escape from."

"I don't doubt you will." Jack kneeled to keep eye contact with the man, feeling a modicum of respect for him. "Why did you drag me all the way out here? There's no place to hide out in open space, especially from me."

"Why does it matter?"

"After all the shit I've been through these last few weeks, it matters a lot."

Larik looked at Allie behind him then back at him and grunted. "After I heard that the council hired you to apprehend me, I knew it was just a matter of time before you caught up with me." He sighed, "Death is the only way to escape you... is what I've been told." Larik ran his thumb over his lip in thought. "I ditched my syndicate and left my second in command in charge. I figured I could spare them at least."

"Cut the crap. I don't care about your underground kingdom. Why did you take us out to the fringes?" Jack needed to know, something uncomfortable ticked at the back of his thoughts.

"My brother."

"Your brother?" Allie asked, stepping forward.

Larik lifted his gaze back to her. "When did you get a girl, Jack?"

Jack cocked his gun and pointed it at his head. "Answer her."

"My brother's ship disappeared out here about six years ago. Never had the time to come out and investigate. But since I was on a countdown... it seemed like the right time to do it." The pirate trailed off, still looking at Allie. "You've seen it, haven't you?" He sat up, hope glistened in his eyes.

Jack interrupted. "We encountered a battlecruiser. Crashed and dead on the planet's surface, Argo, most likely hit by a meteor shower like we were; there were no survivors."

"What about her?" His eyes had yet to move from Allie.

"I was the only survivor," she whispered.

Jack had a headache brewing behind his eyes as Larik sized her up. "No one else survived. The ship is gone, it's deep beneath the planet's surface and in crumbles – *fuck*, it's probably been eaten at this point." Larik ignored him and questioned Allie, angering him.

"Why were you on my brother's battlecruiser?"

"He–he was transporting myself and others."

An awkward silence stifled the air as a thick tension settled in. Larik's jaw ticked, his fists clenching and unclenching. Allie barely breathed as the silence continued. Jack closed his eyes and willed the pounding in his head away.

The pirate turned his gaze back toward him. "You are certain there are no other survivors?"

"There were no other survivors," he heard himself say, unsure why he cared enough to answer.

A long, exhausted sigh escaped from the pirate as he leaned back into the wall, his head tipped up, his eyes closing.

Jack hit the intercom screen and shut the brig with a bang.

• • • •

"JACK, WE NEED TO TALK." She looked over at him staring at the wall where the brig had just been. Her Cyborg turned toward her with a wince.

"We do."

She followed him as he led them into the cockpit.

"What happens now?" She watched as he unhooked the gun attached to his arm and set it aside. She wanted to stay, she knew she could, but she wanted to hear it from his lips again.

The rubble of Larik's ship caught her eye and she walked over to the view screen to examine the pieces floating in space. The tiny pieces of metal that flaked off sparkled in the starlight. She watched Jack's reflection approach her in the glass.

His arms snaked around her and pulled her into his armored form. A deep, low voice whispered in her ear, "You love me."

Allie bit her lip as her gaze caught his, their faces overlaid with the nebulous colors and abyss of space. "I love you." She lost her breath as his body tightened around her.

Before she could respond she was forced up against the chilly window and her leggings were yanked down around her knees. His heated fingers gripped her hips as he pushed his way into her.

"This is what happens next." He grunted as he encased her and his hands moved over hers and plastered them to the cold glass. Her forehead rested on the barrier before her as she braced for his thrusts; her toes came off the ground as he claimed her with each breath. "I love you too."

He took her hard until his desperation died. He took her until she was sore and her muscles shook from overuse. They ended up curled together on the captain's chair with their clothes, armor, and weapons strewn across the glistening floor.

His fingers brushed through her hair as they relaxed into the calm afterglow.

"We need to leave. The distress beacon will have been picked up by others before we arrived."

"Where are we going? To take the pirate in?" she asked.

"Yeah. It'll take a few days." He strapped them in.

"Okay." She smiled, relaxing for the first time in years as Jack blasted the ship into space. She could live like this. Live in the moment with him. They didn't need plans as long as they were together.

• • • •

SEVERAL DAYS HAD GONE by without incident and the further away they got from the *'Hell-in-Space'*, the lighter the mood became. Allie spent most of her time looking at the stars and practicing how to handle his weapons. She also ate a lot. He found her often punching in random codes on his food replicator to try new cuisines. He would have done the same if he had been deprived of real food for half a decade.

Dropping Pirate Captain Larik on Taggert was bittersweet, to say the least. He had grown fond of the quiet, reserved pirate. Probably because he had never spoken after that first day. Allie had remained in the cockpit when he took him off board and delivered him to the Earthian Council guards. The bounty was instantly wired to his account. Soon after, the news of the infamous pirate's capture flooded the intergalactic networks and he had requests coming in for his service from hundreds of sectors.

He had Allie choose their next contract, equipping her with a personal computer that had a list of requests, criminals, and a separate list of missing persons to review and choose from. They had enough money to last a lifetime, even with the repairs to his ship setting them back.

They had uninstalled the salvaged pieces and jettisoned them out into deep space, hoping that no one would ever encounter the strange metal again. A heavy burden left them with the pieces gone.

Now he found himself at a loss, his thoughts drifted off and he ended up picturing Allie. He always ended up there. Before he knew it, he was searching her out as he fantasized about what he wanted to do to her.

Jack located her in the gazer's loft above the circular atrium, lying on her back and gazing at the vast, twinkling space.

She smiled as he settled next to her.

"Under the stars?" she giggled, a lightness in her voice that hadn't been there previously.

"Under every star," he corrected.

"There's a lot of stars."

"Then we better get started." He leaned in and kissed her.

Epilogue:

• • • •

H is cheek was stuck and prickles of ice-needles stabbed his skin as he lifted his face slowly off the cold, stygian ground. A silvery layer of frost expanded out from where he had been lying, creating a beautiful, intricate masterpiece etched across the floor. The silhouette of his form was devoid of its effect.

He would have savored the beauty, being a lover of the arts, if he weren't neck deep in a shitty situation. His hands stuck to the floor as he lifted away, the cold metal pulled at his luke-warm skin.

The breath he released blasted out before his face into a wispy, milky cloud as his mouth frosted over with his saliva. He continuously wet his lips, only for them to harden and chap a moment later.

He was fucking cold.

The air howled, screeching with violent gusts as crystalline flakes of snow blustered through a doorway, and he lifted his face toward the hollow sound. His eyes cleared as they adjusted to the freezing atmosphere.

He was in a metal cube, an iced over jail cell. The ceiling and walls were a tombstone grey that was nearing black. A metallic odor filled his nostrils and it smelled cold, if cold had a smell.

The only thing in the icebox besides himself was a decrepit frame of a bed, the metal bars encased in ice and the bedding long gone.

On unsteady feet, he tested out his legs and his head pounded with the effort.

He couldn't feel the tips of his fingers nor the edges of his ears; his hair fell in sharp icicles around his shoulders, strands of it splintering and breaking off.

He watched as a golden-grey lock dropped to the ground and shattered.

I'm going to die if I don't move.

A wave of wind rang through the space as another deluge of snowflakes blew by, and that was when he noticed the doorway to his room was open. Beyond was an endless sea of white.

His lids grew heavy as his eyelashes hardened. He peeked through the slits to protect his pupils as he took a step forward. His boots crunched over the frosted floor, the sound foreign to his ears. His feet felt heavy with the effort of movement; they were blocks of frozen leather curled around his numb limbs.

He stood right before the passage, unsure if he should continue. The frame of his exit looked like glistening black tears. He tensed his hand and dug his cold nails into his palm but he didn't feel their stab, the appendage devoid of sensation.

He closed his eyes and took an icy breath, accepting the burden of his choices, the choices he had made to end up here at this moment. He regretted nothing.

Larik stepped through the barrier of frozen tears and into an alabaster Hell.

Turn the page to check out what happened to Ophelia and the events leading up to Last Call.

Chapter One:
Collector of Souls

Ophelia ran.

Every fiber of her being screamed in agony. That agony wasn't from the exertion of her straining movements but from the brutality of recent events. If she could run far enough, for long enough, she may be able to outrun the horrors directly behind her. The piercing pain between her legs or the vulnerability and betrayal she felt. Still felt.

The overwhelming disappointment that had quickly become horrendous struggles and screams.

If she could run far enough, for long enough it could be buried in her past. But it was so painfully part of her present that no amount of movement was going to make it go away.

She could still feel the rough hands holding her down, biting into her skin, where minutes before they had been removed and clinical. The calluses of those hands, a sharp contrast to her soft skin, rubbing it raw like bark.

Ophelia diverted off the dirt path and into the darkening forest. The sun was setting directly behind her, casting a bloody twilight across the landscape; the sound of pursuers long gone. They had given up long ago but she still felt them right behind her.

A torn sheath of a dress fluttered behind her as she ran deeper into the woods. The trees around her scraped at her skin as she flung her body through the low hanging branches; the bushes snagged the flimsy cloth of her dress, further ripping the material's hem.

What did I do that made me unworthy of being fertile? She sobbed.

The doctors– the priests of her colony had initiated the ritual of her womanhood just hours ago. She had reached an age where her protectors could no longer ensure her safety, especially with the possibility that she may be fertile. It was a good possibility, too, as her mother was Earthian and had brought forth several children.

I was suppose to bring forth children.

Her protectors, the barren women who managed the traveling orphanages, released their guardianship of her as the ritual commenced and delivered her to the temple of their gods. If she was deemed fertile, Ophelia would have been transported to one of their colony's communes and if she were deemed barren she would have been left to fend for herself– thrown to the wolves of their feudal world.

The morning brought dread and excitement and it had overpowered her psyche. It had been her dream to rise in the ranks of the Warlord's regime and to be paired off with a great warrior, to bring strong children into this world. *That* was the world she had been raised in, always aware of the power that she could have but also of the danger.

If she was fertile, she would suddenly become a treasure, a *prize*. She could be kidnapped or held against her will, hurt, or even killed. But if the laws of the land protected her with the strong fist of the Warlord's might, she would have been powerful and protected.

Breeders were rare.

On the other hand, if she was found to be barren, Ophelia would have no rights, no protection, and would be left to fend for herself. She could still be hurt, kept against her will, or even killed, but no one would care or come to her aid.

She would just be another mouth, and in such a blood-possessed colony where resources were limited, science and technology had come to a screeching halt; the constant harvest of diseased, inedible crops, there were very few professions she could do to take care of herself.

She may have found a husband, like some of the barren women did, but she would only have the protection of a man who was not a warrior and would not be able to protect her like a warrior could.

And a hybrid like herself would not go unnoticed by the men.

The thought of becoming a concubine, blindingly aware of the stabbing pain between her legs, made her gut wrench. *I will never give myself to a man now.*

Ophelia gasped, her lungs burned with the heavy weight of overexertion, ready to collapse. Her foot caught a root; it twisted her leg beneath her and sent her crashing to the ground as an ominous beat of wings sounded overhead, heralding the coming of darkness.

She looked around while the panic and adrenaline still coursed through her veins, keeping her going. The need to outrun the priests had been her sole motivation, but now that the day was fading into eventide she needed a new goal.

Her time in the light was coming to an end and the dense forest was impenetrable at night. *I need to find shelter– a place to hide.*

Lost time could never be restored.

Dragging her body over the bristly ground, her hands sunk into the moist, slippery soil as she bore herself forward. The dirt and mud drenched her thin, torn dress, and it left her cold and shivering.

She crawled on all fours deeper into the gloom, hyperaware of every sound around her. The crunch of leaves under her knees, the beat of wings high above her head, the distant howl of an animal. Ophelia's ears twitched with every noise as she focused on discerning any sound of pursuers, whether it was of male voices or the tell-tale broken twig.

Why have I become nothing? I'm a blight, a bad seed, and now a lost innocent. They were so sure I would be sent to the female commune but now I'm nothing. Her fingers clawed at her chest.

Ophelia miscalculated her grip and tumbled over a hidden ledge where she rolled down a steep incline until her fall was broken with a painful crack. Her body was pressed against a long, rough root sticking out of the ground.

Moaning, she curled herself into a fetal position to ride out terrible waves of pain. Her eyes clenched tight with shock as she took inventory of her form; her shaking hand felt around and located a dull protrusion over her ribs and, as Ophelia explored the break, the sharp bone punctured her skin, she battled roils of torment and was dragged into unconsciousness. Her hand fell away, bloody.

It wasn't until the last golden ray of light flashed and lit up behind her eyelids that she lifted her gaze to her new surroundings.

A giant, gnarled tree loomed before her like a monstrous obstruction.

It was shaded by the fading light that crested in a ruby halo around its form. She had to hood her eyes to see it clearly as a distorted shadow towered out toward her, growing longer with every second. The wispy darkness of it clawed its way over the sodden ground and she knew she would be engulfed by it at any moment.

Giant, lumbering roots burst from the thick trunk and spread out in every direction; Ophelia's small, broken form was plastered against one.

The tree looked like a nightmare and she was equally intrigued and awed by its wild beauty. When she began to catch her breath, she could smell a rich, terra musk.

I'm so ugly. I would do anything to be that dark and beautiful. She wiped the back of her hand across her cheek.

Ophelia felt compelled to crawl closer to the trunk, maneuvering her way through the large, winding roots; *wanting* to get closer to it. When she was at the innermost apex, she leaned her bruised back into the rigid bark and pulled her legs up to her body.

The tree provided her protection but it did not provide her warmth.

As her heart rate slowed and her breathing eased, the pain and memories of her torn, beaten innocence came back in full force. She willed it to go away with all of her might and tried instead to focus on what was before her now.

That she was cold and raw, a husk of the girl she had been just hours before but she was alive, alone, and away from her abusers.

Blood flooded down from between her legs to pool and soak into the moist dirt below her. She could feel the sanguine leave her as every new gush was another piece of her innocence gone. *My blood is dirty, I want it gone.* She wrapped her arms around herself and shook.

The priests had held her down and took turns with her body as she screamed and sobbed to no avail. The old, decrepit men were eerily unconcerned with her pain, and drowned out her cries with grunts of their own.

She hated them. If she had the chance or the ability she would avenge herself and kill them all. *To hell with the Xanteaus and gods of this world.* The tree was her only god now.

Ophelia was overcome with rage, with her pain, and with the despair of being utterly alone.

I want to kill them; all of them. I want to rip their innocence away like they ripped mine. I want my hands to be dripping with their blood as I bathe in their screams.

A dark, hellish stream of thoughts bombarded her mind. They took her breath away and filled her with fire. The shadows of the gnarled branches above her cast a blood-black shadow over her form, hiding her from the light.

I would do anything to have the life I was promised.
I would sell my soul.

She felt an abrupt shift in the air. The cold evening chill pulsed away from her as a numbing sensation descended in its place. She was left alone with her frenetic emotions as the void around her grew heavier. The sounds of the forest faded away.

Ophelia closed her eyes tightly and wished–

Please. If you can hear me, any deity, any god that will listen. Please answer my wish. I have lost everything and I want it back. BACK.

"Are you sure you want it back?" A deep, hissed whisper came from the darkness before her.

She opened her eyes in shock and stared into the black nothingness, trying to locate the source of the strange voice. Had something answered?

"Who's there?" she called weakly, her throat sore from earlier events.

"The one you wished for."

Her mouth parted and she licked her lips as she tried to understand the significance of the answer. "You heard me? How is that possible?" She rasped dryly. The shadows before her were thick and impenetrable.

"You wished for me. And now I'm here." The low voice was sensuous. "Unless you would like me to leave?"

She prickled with foreboding. The voice didn't sound human. What deity had answered her pathetic call? "Don't– don't leave. Who did I summon?" she asked again.

A long quiet pause fell between her and the shadows. The entity in the forest became so silent that she thought that it had left. Her foot sank into the mud as she swiped a damp, stray strand of her hair off her face and sat forward.

A deep, stabbing pain shot through her weakening body. It coursed from between her legs to the tips of her fingers– to the end of her toes.

"You're dying." The mysterious man hummed.

She couldn't see clearly anymore, the rays of the setting sun had dissipated; her only source of light now was from the silvery moonbeams of the stars. They morphed the scarlet glen into a dimming silver-bullet grey. It was then she noticed the black pool of blood spreading around her body.

I'm bleeding out. The entity had diagnosed her imminent death.

"Can you save me?" She croaked softly. *Do I want to be saved?* Now that she knew she was on the precipice of death, Ophelia felt a heavy pressure ease from her soul. She never realized how life itself could bear down so strongly that the gateway of death would be welcomed with its lightened load.

The shivers that ran down her spine were ones of anxiety rather than cold. *The deity will either save me or I will die.* Either option was better than continuing on in the broken existence she was currently treading.

"I can."

"How?"

"We make a trade." It answered softly. The voice had a hint of eagerness to it now.

"What do we trade?" Ophelia knew. Deep down, she knew; but she needed to hear it.

"Your soul." The dark voice stated with a stern finality.

Thoughts raced through her mind. She was weak and lightheaded from the blood loss. Could insanity be a part of death? She had run long and far, fleeing from the monsters that chased her, but she never thought that running from them would lead her right into the clutches of another, more sinister being. *Is my mind as broken as my body?*

Her thoughts were so painfully lucid. She couldn't be going crazy.

"You're not crazy." The entity answered her as if it read her mind.

A wave of dizziness enveloped her. Her body twitched with electric jerks as she hunched over and clutched her head, forcing her mind to ground itself. The world spun around her as a death-like weakness gripped her body.

Ophelia could feel the cold hands of the reaper caress her dirty skin. She weakly looked up with her waning strength and addressed the darkness.

"If I give you my soul..." she trailed off as she briefly lost her train of thought. "You would give me back my innocence?" She swallowed, "My life? You would make me fertile?"

"Yes." It answered quickly.

"Why?" She asked in disbelief, wondering how her soul could be worth so much.

"Power."

Power?

"Who are you?" Her arms curled around her knees as she watched the forest line, looking for the entity.

Once again silence descended in the vale. She knew her time was coming to an end as her face grew heavy, her muscles twitched with weakness as the world around her started to fade to grey. Right as she began to close her lids and succumb to oblivion, a slight movement caught her eye.

She conjured enough willpower to lift her eyelids for the figure beyond her sight. Ophelia wanted to see the deity that had answered her call, if it was the last thing that would occur in her life.

Shadows oozed from the wood like muddy water slipping across silk to solidify into a tall figure at the tree-line. The gloom fell into wavering, yet lucid shapes until it formed into the figure of a man. He wore the darkness like a cloak around his form and made the twilight look like day with how bleak he was.

The man's face was hidden behind an aura of obscurity; the only feature she could discern was the mischievous sparkle of his hooded yellow eyes.

Was she really considering giving her soul in exchange for getting everything she wanted? Deserved?

Yes.

As if he read her thoughts, the mysterious being stepped forward. He made no sound but the dull thump and crunch of his steps. She hadn't realized that she was holding her breath until he stopped to tower over her huddled form.

"What will you do with me?" She asked softly, frightened of the unknown presence and yet strangely intrigued.

"Nothing." He paused, his voice deep. "When you die, I will collect payment. Until then, I will grant your requests and then I will leave."

"But... my soul?"

"Will be mine. To do with as I please for the rest of eternity."

A shiver of doubt tugged at her. She couldn't quite believe that this was anything more than a bad dream. Could she surrender eternity? Her mind grew weak at the thought, and her remaining strength bled out to join her lost innocence in the soil.

The dark figure crouched before her and peered into her eyes. The shade around his face lifted away to reveal an unholy visage. Her mouth parted open in disbelief.

He is the most beautiful thing I have ever seen.

Mesmerized, Ophelia leaned toward him involuntarily.

"Shall we seal the deal with a kiss?" He asked as he lifted his hand to stroke her tear-stained cheek. His fingers were warm to the touch.

"Yes." She breathed. *I would sell my soul to kiss you.*

He dazzled her with an indulgent smile. Blazing hands cupped her neck as his thumbs tilted her chin up. He leaned forward to place a soft, chaste kiss upon her pale lips. The touch electrified her senses.

The feel of his mouth over hers was the last thing Ophelia remembered before she slipped into a dreamless, void-like sleep.

Click here[1] to continue the story...

Author's Note:

. . . .

Thank you for reading my first book, I hope you liked reading it as much as I loved writing it! If you enjoyed my book please leave me an honest review on Amazon or Goodreads. You can reach me at my facebook page NaomiLucasRomance for updates and announcements about future installments or you can join my newsletter[1]!

Naomi Lucas

---

1. https://app.mailerlite.com/webforms/landing/j1n6p0

About the Author

Naomi Lucas is an indie author who is struggling to navigate the intricacies of social media. She loves being creative whether its with painting, writing, or making little jingles about her dog, Barracuda, or her cat, Daliah, in the car.

But more importantly, she is a coffee addict with a lustful, burning desire to visit the Starbucks Factory in Seattle and never leave.

Read more at https://naomilucasauthor.com/.

Made in the USA
Las Vegas, NV
24 June 2022

50665450R00146